THE TROUBLESOME YEARS

James A. Pounds

THE TROUBLESOME YEARS is a novel describing the troubles of families that lived through the years after the Civil War and of the Great Depression of the 1920s and 1930s and the war years of the 1940s, 1950s, and 1960s.

Those were very trying times for America and most of the world. World War II was the greatest catastrophe the world had ever known. Never had the people of the world been so completely involved in fighting, genocide, and murder. Every country on the globe was involved in the war and none were untouched by the anxieties and hardships of that conflict. Many millions died because of their religion or place of birth. Civilians died by the thousands; those innocents, caught up in the fighting between the warring nations.

Copyright © 2012

James A. Pounds

ALL RIGHTS RESERVED

No portion of this publication may be reproduced, stored in any electronic system, or transmitted in any form or by any means, electronic, mechanical, photocopy, recording or otherwise, without written permission from the author. Brief quotations may be used in literary reviews.

This is a work of fiction. It is not meant to depict, portray or represent any particular real persons. All of the characters are the products of the author's imagination and are not to be construed as real. Any references or similarities to actual events, entities, real people, living or dead, or to characters, entities, and incidents are entirely coincidental.

ISBN 13: 978-1460951231

ISBN 10: 1460951239

Second Edition

Other titles by James A. Pounds

- *The Story of Our War*
- *Operation Borneo* *(co-author)*

DEDICATION

This volume is dedicated to my daughter, Jeanette A. Pounds, who has been supportive of my desire to write and for her help in editing the entire work.

I wish to thank Jennifer Sugarman for providing special technical assistance in preparing the manuscript.

This book is dedicated also

to the many families who struggled through the early years of the Depression in the late 1920s and to those families who were devastated by the closing of the banks and the ensuing deeper Depression of the mid-1930s

and

to those who lost loved ones in the war years of the 1940s and 1950s and to all of those who endured The Troublesome Years, for they were heroes.

James A. Pounds

TABLE OF CONTENTS

Foreword

Introduction

Chapter One: The Civil War Years... 1

Chapter Two: Reconstruction Period.. 5

Chapter Three: World Conditions 11

Chapter Four: The Will Smith Family 17

Chapter Five: The Noles Family 85

Chapter Six: The Barnes Family.. 127

Chapter Seven: The Hairston Family 133

Chapter Eight: The Anthony DiCarlo Family...................... 137

Chapter Nine: Arthur... 145

Chapter Ten: The Model T Ford... 155

Epilogue   163

FOREWORD

THE TROUBLESOME YEARS starts with the trying times after the War of 1812 and the following depression years of the 1830s, through the 1850s, then with the families that made it through the Civil War and the difficult years that followed during the Reconstruction Period.

A poor subsistence farm family's story is told, about how they coped with the Great Depression in the 1930s and what effect the failure of the stock market had on them.

There is the story of a farm family of means, who, by all normal circumstances should have been able to withstand the fall of the stock market and possibly the closing of the banks. This family was overwhelmed by the total lack of a market for their farm products. They might have survived and held onto their lands if the banks had not failed in 1932. Their money in the bank would have been sufficient to pay off the mortgage. Not all of their large acreage was mortgaged, so this made it possible for the family to make a good living on the remaining portion of the original estate. During the war years they contributed grandsons to the war effort in both the 1940s and 1950s.

An African-American couple is the subject of another portion of the book and how they coped with the tough times. Segregation in the southern states made the possibility for meaningful employment for the black population almost impossible except as day labor or domestic help. As for the majority, they were not directly affected by the stock market crash. The closing of the banks was of little or no concern to this segment of society or to the poorer white population, for most of them had any bank accounts. This group also contributed sons to both World War II and the Korean War.

The last family story tells of an immigrant family that came from their ancestral home in Italy, seeking a new world in which to start their married life. This family knew full well the hardships of a depressed economy. They were looking to make their way in a new country that was, at the time, a prosperous nation. The family did well in the early years before World War I. After the war, as the economy began to fail in the 1920s, the head of the household was still able to keep a job and provide for his family. This family also provided a son for the war in the 1940s.

EPILOGUE is a brief summary of the start of World War II. Early conquests of the Japanese forces are detailed to show what happened in the Southwest Pacific immediately after the bombing of Pearl Harbor, Hawaii. Details and timing are shown to illustrate how long it took for the United States and the Allied Forces to respond to the Japanese aggression in the Pacific. The action taken by the Allied Forces indicates how difficult the task of stopping the enemy was in the early years of the war. A detail of the results of the war in cost of lives taken during the war years is given to show the effect on the families that survived the Great Depression. Some serious thought has been given to the number of casualties that would have been incurred if there had been an invasion of the Japanese homeland. Details of the planned invasion operation are outlined to show what would have happened if the war had not ended after the second atomic bomb was dropped on Nagasaki, Japan.

War and turmoil did not really end after the Japanese forces surrendered. It continued sporadically in many parts of the world. When the major war ended, the indigenous people of the colonies of France, the Netherlands and the British Empire located in the Southwest Pacific began to demand independence from their oppressive overlords. These colonies had been ruled by the major powers of Europe for a long time and they now wanted their independence and were willing to fight if necessary.

The native leaders of the colonies knew that the European powers were profiting greatly by confiscating their natural resources. The islands were rich in iron ore, tin, manganese, gold, rubber and timber. The natives wanted and demanded that their commodities be freed from the control of outside interests.

As soon as the war ended, the natives of Borneo demanded the Dutch leave the island and forfeit any claim they had on the oil reserves of the area.

This is the plan of attack on the main island of Japan that would have taken place if the Japanese did not cease fighting and accept the peace plan of the Allied Forces. Fortunately the plan did not have to be used.

INTRODUCTION

The primary purpose of writing this novel was to relate some of the author's firsthand knowledge of the Great Depression years. Growing up during the post-World War I years, he was well aware of the Great Depression and the effects of the crash of the stock market in 1929. During the worst years of the Depression, he was a teenager going to high school. Shortly after his twenty-first birthday, Pearl Harbor was bombed. He became a soldier in the United States Army and fought in World War II.

A review of the early history of the United States indicates that depressions and cyclical poverty have been problems in the past. After the Civil War and after the bitter years of Reconstruction, there were problems with labor unions. Then came the recovery after 1900 and the economy revived until the end of World War I. During World War II there were fifteen million young men and women in the military service. The war solved some of the problems of unemployment. Production of war materials and equipment put every available person in the work force. The Great Depression and massive unemployment may have continued for many more years if the war had not occurred. In comparing the economy today with that of the 1930s, there are many similarities commencing in 2008 when the economy began to fail early in the year. The stock market fell 6000 points in just a few days and businesses began to lay off employees. Banks and financial firms went bankrupt. Before the year was out, unemployment had reached the 10% level. Auto plants were going bankrupt, laying off hundreds of employees.

The newly-elected President began to throw billions of dollars of government money to the large banking firms and the automobile industry. His thought in doing so was that it would benefit the economy and that the country could not allow the large firms to go under. No thought was given at the time to make provisions for solving the unemployment problem. Big banks and the auto industry were slowly reviving but sales were poor all year. Many of the mortgaged homes were worth much less at the end of the year than they were mortgaged for when purchased. The deflation of home prices made it difficult to sell property and it required the mortgagee to make higher payments on a home that was deflated 50% in value from the original price.

The downturn in the economy, the high rate of unemployment and the drastic drop in consumer spending caused income in the form of taxes to drop accordingly. Rather than reduce spending, states and counties began increasing taxes, and even to invent new forms of revenue. The cost of many licenses permits and such were increased. For some, there were increases of up to 400%. One state increased the cost of driver's licenses from ten dollars to forty dollars. Automobile tags were increased 140%. Sales tax and unemployment tax for business owners was increased, which caused even more unemployment. Institutions became insolvent due to their greed and mismanagement. Large firms were granting millions of dollars in bonuses to their top echelon managers while the company was going bankrupt. At the same time the government was providing the corporations with billions of dollars in loans to prevent their bankruptcy. In recent years, they had adopted poor lending practices, gorging themselves with mortgages that were based on poor credit of the buyers and inflated prices for the properties. The banks were dealing heavily in derivate paper that was being traded daily.

Beginning after the turn of the century in 2000, a great push was made by the banks to increase credit card debt. Credit cards were being given out to just about everyone who requested them. Many of the credit card holders did not realize the cost of their debt. Banks were making millions as long as the card holders could pay the high interest on their balances. As the economy began to fail and unemployment became rampant in 2008, many card holders could not make their monthly payments. The banks sat holding millions of dollars of debt.

The large lending agencies were granting mortgages to persons with no down payments and with no credit checks. To help the home buyer get a mortgage they provided two years of low monthly interest payments. After the two years, the interest rate would be increased by up to 4%, making it impossible for many buyers to make the higher monthly payments. Homes began to be foreclosed by the thousands each month. Even the Fannie Mae government approved Mortgage Corporation was in a position of bankruptcy due to an excessive number of failed home loans.

The three large auto firms were at the brink of failure due to poor management, loss of sales from overseas competition, and the unemployment situation. The government loaned them millions of dollars in order for them to reorganize and become viable businesses again. With the coming of the new year of 2009, there was some relief but unemployment continued to rise. Loans for business operation and expansion were not available. Banks were unwilling to loan money until the economy improved. Many banks continued to close their doors.

Local and state governments, desperate for tax revenue, increased the cost of car tags and driver's licenses. They even passed a law to require a fishing license in order for anyone to fish with a cane pole in a creek or on the beach. There seemed no limit to what would be taxed next. The legislature made a pretense of cutting real estate taxes but their brilliant scheme was: after reducing the tax by 3%, they increased the taxable assessed value of the property by 10%, so the taxes went up anyway. It would seem that during a depression the government should cut down on wasteful and discretionary spending and lower taxes to ease the burden on the unemployed.

As the year of 2010 began, we heard the politicians saying loud and clear that what we need is more jobs, but we didn't see much being done about unemployment. When President Roosevelt took office in the 1930s, he moved very quickly to create jobs. Government projects were put into motion immediately to offer work to the unemployed. The current political group in office was quick to bail out the greedy banks and lending institutions but they did nothing to alleviate unemployment. Politicians now are following the philosophy of President Hoover with his idea that private enterprise should provide for the unemployed. He thought that the government should not have to fund projects to put the unemployed back to work.

Chapter One

The Civil War Years

Zechariah Wilson was the youngest of ten children. He was born in 1862 just before his father, Isaac Wilson, enlisted in the 3rd Alabama Infantry Regiment. Three of his brothers, John, Benjamin and Joseph had enlisted in the 5th Alabama Artillery Battalion and his other brother, Elijah, was already in the Confederate Army at the time the hostilities of the Civil War began.

Isaac Wilson had migrated to central Alabama as a young man from eastern Tennessee. He married a local farmer's daughter and settled on a homestead of 80 acres of bottomland along Caney Creek. His land adjoined his father-in-law's estate on the north side. His first order of activity on his property was to build a dam on the creek, then build a mill house, and install a water wheel that would drive a sawmill, a grist mill and a forge hammer. The mill would provide good income for the family for years.

Times were hard following the war of 1812. The economy declined in the 1820s and 1830s. In addition to the other troubles during these years, there was no stable currency. Paper money issued by the government was basically worthless and it was referred to as not being worth a "continental damn". Silver and gold were the only money that had any value, and were very hard to obtain.

The 1840s were plagued by political upheaval over the matter of slavery. The Northern factions in Washington D.C. wanted slavery abolished but the Southern members of Congress insisted they must have slave labor in order to maintain their agricultural economy. During this decade the price of farm products dropped to almost nothing and there was no market for them.

Letter from Isaac Wilson's brother in Tennessee in the 1840s:

Dear Isaac: Besides it being a pleasure it seems my duty to write to my brother and send news of our family. I also feel it's my duty to write to you because you last wrote to me and asked that I stay in touch. I hope that when mine comes to hand you and your family will be doing well. My family and I are doing well and all the connections as far as I know. I am still living in Bedford. Times are still hard and if it is getting better as some are inclined to think it is so slow that to me it is improbable. There is no market at all for tobacco; cotton is worth about six dollars per bale in Nashville. Pork is worth two dollars per hundred pounds. Corn is only worth ten cents per bushel, wheat is seventy five cents per bushel and horses and all other property is very low. Traders that carried off horses in the early fall did well but of late they did badly. We have very little hope of revival. Alabama money will only pass at twenty per cent discount and as our State Bank is to resume specie* payment shortly it is thought that it will depreciate.. I may mention that there are many doubts into our bank holding up. I am tempted to apply for the benefits of the Bankruptcy Law for I am sorry Tennessee musters a legion in that department. You will not fail to write when you get this letter. Your Brother, William.

Although the economy of the country was down and markets for farm produce were almost non-existent, Isaac did well. He was producing flour and corn meal in his grist mill and his pay was a portion of the grain that he processed. His forge was making the tools that were needed for farming, logging and home construction. Iron nails were always in demand and he was making them in his forge using "bog iron" that was found along creek banks in northern Alabama. Every day the saw mill operated producing lumber to build houses. Smooth lumber was an everyday need for the builders for most people no longer lived in log cabins.

*specie refers to money backed by gold or silver

The economy did not improve much in the 1850s. There was growing turmoil over the question of slavery, especially in the new territories of Kansas and Missouri where the people wanted statehood. The Abolitionists wanted the territories to become free states and the Southerners wanted the states to have a choice where slavery could exist. By the end of the decade, there was much fervor in Washington over the slavery issues and there was a threat in Congress by the representatives of the Southern states that they might secede from the Union if slavery were abolished.

In the early 1860s the Southern states did secede and the Civil war began. Nearly every man, young and old, in the Southern states joined the Confederate army. Isaac Wilson's sons were some of the first to join up. Isaac himself joined up in the second year of the war. In the spring of 1865, the war ended with General Robert E. Lee's surrender at the Appomattox Courthouse in Virginia.

President Abraham Lincoln signed the Emancipation Proclamation in 1863, freeing all slaves and now that the war was over, where would they go? How would they live and provide for themselves? Those were most troublesome times for the freed slaves. Could they remain on the plantations where they had lived and worked before, and work for the owner as free men? Some of them did just that. They were set up as share-croppers, provided with a piece of land and a house, and they paid their rent by working for the land owner. Many of the newly free men moved north where the people were more sympathetic with their cause and their current needs. Others moved to the Western territories seeking a new start in a new land.

Isaac and his sons were fortunate to have made it through the war and return home. John had been captured by the Yankees and was imprisoned at Liberty Prison until the war was over. After the surrender, he was released from prison and he returned home. There was no transportation for released prisoners and John had to walk all the way home from Ohio, to his home in central Alabama.

When the Wilson men returned home after the war, they found that their dam on Caney Creek had been breached. Most of the mill had been destroyed when the Yankee soldiers passed through Isaac's property. The soldiers had taken all of the livestock they could find. Isaac's wife and the other women had hidden what animals they could in the thick cane break by the creek before the soldiers arrived at the farm. While the men were fighting, the women took care of plowing the fields sowing the crops and harvesting. They sheared the sheep for the wool and processed it into yarn in order to make warm clothing.

Food was provided by slaughtering the hogs, preserving the meat and storing it in the smoke house. Their cheese, butter and milk came from the cows. They cultivated a large garden plot the year around in order to have fresh vegetables. Those women were self-sufficient and able to provide quite well for their own needs.

After the close of the war the entire South was invaded by "carpetbaggers" and Union soldiers who were looking to steal and pilfer anything of value. Immediately after the end of hostilities the Union soldiers went about taking or destroying anything they could find.

While the three women were in the cane break down by the creek guarding the cattle, they witnessed the soldiers going through the house seeking anything of value they could find. Then the soldiers went to the barn and spilled out the grain barrels and caught up as many chickens as they could carry back to their camp. As the soldiers left the house they took bolts of "linsey-woolsey" cloth, tied it to their saddle horns and let the material fly in the wind as they rode away.

The soldiers and the carpet baggers were a serious menace after the war. Things were so bad that one family killed several carpet baggers while they were attempting to steal the family livestock. After the family disposed of the thieves they loaded all their possessions in wagons and the entire family moved out and went to Arkansas. Many families left the South after the war to escape the harsh punishment from the Union soldiers who were stationed there to keep the peace and maintain order.

Chapter Two

Reconstruction Period - 1865-1870s

With the close of the Civil War, the Southern states were in utter chaos for the remainder of the 1860s. Union soldiers were stationed throughout the South to enforce the new laws placed upon the Southern states. Ex-slaves were given the right to vote. Southerners were denied the vote unless they signed a pledge of allegiance to the Union. Carpetbaggers and ex-Union soldiers roamed the entire South seeking to rob anyone they could and take anything they could carry away. As if the times were not hard enough, these conditions made things even worse. Most families in the South had lost fathers, sons, brothers and husbands during the conflict and many women and children had to provide for the families.

The days of Reconstruction in the South (as the Yankees referred to the last half of the 1860s and the 1870s) were over by 1880. In the South those were, indeed, troublesome years.

The Southern economy had been completely destroyed by the war and the years that followed, as a result of the harsh treatment imposed by the Union Forces. In the 1880s, the economy of the whole country was commencing to recover. The plantations of the South were again producing large cotton crops and there was a great need for cotton in Europe. Corn and grain were being produced in large quantities for the northern market. Manufacturing of steel and durable goods was going strong in the Northern states and everyone felt that at last things were improving and the economy was returning to normal.

The railroads were expanding and were being built across the western territory, all the way to the Pacific coast of California. Steel mills were working full time to produce rails for the new tracks. There were steady markets for iron and steel for construction and manufacturing.

Things in the economy were looking good with the beginning of the 1890s, but in the South there was a deep freeze in the weather and for three years it was difficult to do any farming without major crop loss. Then the North began feeling a letdown in the growth of the economy. There were strikes in the coal mines, the steel mills and with the transportation suppliers. The workers were demanding to have unions to represent them in negotiations with the mill and mine owners for better pay and working conditions.

In the early 1870s, John Wilson and his brother Joe migrated to the Gulf Coast in Mississippi. John taught school in Jackson County. Joe obtained a small farm at Broad Beach, where he established a successful vegetable farm. He shipped vegetables to the northern markets. Here on the Mississippi coast, in the mild winter weather, he was able to grow vegetables the year around. Ben and his family moved from Central Alabama by wagon train to western Texas. In Texas, he acquired a tract of land and become a rancher. Elijah and his family left central Alabama and traveled down the river to Mobile, where the family embarked on a steamer for Baton Rouge, Louisiana. From there they planned to go along the Red River to Arkansas. On the boat trip to Baton Rouge, Elijah contracted cholera and died. He was buried on the bank of the river. His grieving family continued on to Arkansas and established themselves on a small farm in the Ozark Mountains.

Isaac Wilson had ten children, five boys and five girls. The youngest child was Zechariah. He attended the best schools available at the time. He graduated from the High School Academy and then went on to study for the ministry. He and his wife, Lena Martin, were married in 1885. That year, he taught his first school year in a one-room school located on Dauphin Island, at the mouth of Mobile Bay. Most of his life was spent teaching school during the week and then on Sundays, he preached at one of the local churches. Later in life he owned and operated a local newspaper. At various times, he was the county tax assessor, a postmaster and a member of the State Legislature. Of Isaac's ten children, five were born to his first wife who passed away in 1894, and with his second wife, he had five more children.

Lena Wilson's great grandfather, Jonas Martin, migrated from South Carolina, to the fertile valley of Big Mulberry Creek, Alabama, in 1795. At that time white settlers were required to have a permit from the Chief of the ten Creek Nations to live in Indian Territory. Her grandfather had settled on 360 acres of good bottomland along the creek's flood plain when Alabama became a state in 1819. He deeded his son Enoch, Lena's father, 80 acres of land and built him and his wife, Ann Hayes, a log cabin on the property when they were married. This was the home in which Lena and her younger brother, Hugh, was born and grew up.

Enoch Martin enlisted in the 5th Alabama Artillery Battalion when the Civil War began, which left his wife Ann and their two small children to fend for themselves while he was away.

Ann did have some help for there were two slave women that lived on the place, whose husbands went to war with Enoch. During the battle of Shiloh, the 5th Artillery Battalion lost 60% of its men and nearly all of its guns. Enoch and his two slave men were casualties of the battle. Ann was left to raise the two children by herself for she never married again. Her two slave women were freed by Lincoln's Emancipation Proclamation of 1863 but they chose to remain with Ann and the children and help on the farm for their keep. The women were provided with a small but adequate log cabin and they shared in the farm products and what small income that was to be had in the dark days of Reconstruction. They stayed with Ann the rest of their lives.

When Lena passed away, Zechariah was left with five small children the oldest was eight years old and the youngest was six months old. Zechariah was teaching school every day during the week and preaching every Sunday and he needed someone to take care of the children. Willie Sutter was a fellow preacher and he had an old maid sister who came in to care for the children. Within three months, Zechariah and Lutie Sutter were married. Now he had a second wife to provide for, as well as the children. He and Lutie lost no time in

7

starting another family of children for their first child was born nine months after their marriage. Then every two years or so, another baby was born. In all, Lutie had another five children to care for and feed every day. As her children began to arrive she was spending most of her time taking care of her brood and Zechariah's first group of children was being neglected.

Of the ten children, the oldest child was seventeen and the youngest was not quite one year old. There were four boys and one girl in the first family and four boys and one girl in the second. In each group of children the girls were the youngest. By the time Lutie had her second child, she had no time for the first group of children and they became belligerent, unruly and very discouraged. The older boys would spend their days aggravating their stepmother whenever possible in ways such as climbing onto the roof and threatening to jump off. Once they heard that the neighbors down the road had the measles but the boys didn't know what measles were, so they took a bucket with them to see if they could have some. In a few days the entire family was infected.

The three older boys were hired out to a local farmer to work in the fields when they were young teenagers hoeing cotton, thinning corn and plowing. They each earned 25 cents per day for working from sunup to sundown. The money was paid to their father and they never received a cent of their wages. Since they were working, they had no time to go to school and consequently they received very little education. When the three oldest boys were sixteen, eighteen and twenty years old they ran away from home. The youngest joined the Navy by lying about his age. The next son caught a freight train and rode as a hobo to New Orleans. There he found refuge with an older couple who felt sorry for him and took him in, fed him and found him a job in one of the large sawmills in the area. Over time he became an apprentice millwright. He worked at the mill for several years until he came down with malaria and then he chose to return home to recuperate. The older brother also went to New Orleans and was able to sign on with the merchant marines as an apprentice seaman on board a tramp steamer. He spent many years at sea and finally became a ship's captain. The fourth son remained at home. He got a job with the local station master at the railroad depot. He learned to be a telegrapher and remained with the railroad for many years. The youngest child, the daughter, married when she was seventeen to a local subsistence farmer.

Now that the first group of children had left home, Lutie had only her own five children. The oldest child was a deaf mute, requiring extra attention while he was little. Her next oldest son joined the Army and served in World War I. The next two sons joined the Army as they reached eighteen years of age, remaining in the service through World War II. The youngest of the children, the daughter, married a young ex-Army soldier who became an engineer on the railroad. After the children had all left home and married, Zechariah and Lutie passed away within six months of each other when they were in their early sixties.

After the turn of the century, things in the South were looking good for the farmers and the timber merchants. The South was fortunate to have large tracts of virgin pine, oak and other hardwoods. At that time there was a great demand for timber and timber products at home and abroad. Railroads were built especially to haul wood from the inland areas to the shipping ports on the Gulf of Mexico. Large sawmills were built to process the timber as it was hauled to the port areas. For many years until World War I, timber processing was a booming business in the South. Another profitable business associated with the timber industry was the collecting and processing of naval stores, rosin, pine oil and turpentine. These naval products were in demand around the world because they were key materials for shipbuilding and the repair of ships.

Things continued going well until 1915, when Germany decided to start a war in Europe. In the early years of the war, our country said we would not get involved in Europe and send troops but would finance England and France in their fight with Germany. This effort improved the economy of the United States but it became time very soon to send troops to fight in Europe in order to protect the interest that the United States had in financing the war effort of our Allies. The following letter tells of the critical post-war times and the damage South had endured.

October 1865:

Dear Son: I take this opportunity of writing to you again we are all well except your Papa he isn't doing well. Charley, Sidney and Joe are here sitting by the fire. Sis and Penny are at your uncle Thomas's. Sarah and Susan were here last night and they went home with them. They all want you to come home. Your Grandfather wants to see you get home. He was the proudest old man when all my boys came home and all his boys got back alive. Now if you get home it will be something remarkable. It is a great mercy and nothing but the workings of a kind providence that could have done such great things. Bless the Lord for his goodness and kindness towards the children of men.

We received your letter and were glad to hear from you and you wanted to know what we had left. The Rebs took all of our horses except one mare and the Yankees got the mule. It was a first rate mule that we got when we traded Sidney's horse. Sidney has gone to see the Claims Agent and I think he will get paid for the horse.

Now I will tell you what we have left we have all our cattle, sixty head of hogs and about that many sheep. Your Pa bought a good horse last fall for 200 "Cornfed" dollars* but the horse had a sore foot. The foot has now got well and he is a good horse now and he is good at the buggy. We have two buggies and one carriage and all our wagons. I kept the wagons hid out when old Hood's slow train* passed here last they would have taken them to carry the wounded in. They took peoples shop tools but we kept your shop tools by hiding them out. We had to keep all of our clothing hid to keep the Tories from taking them. They plundered homes all about here.

Chapter Three

World Conditions - 1920s, 1930s and 1940s

It was cold and wet that spring of 1921, in Alabama. It looked as if warm weather would be a very late in coming. Times were hard for World War I had only been over for three short years and the world economy had not recovered from the devastation of the industrial might of Europe. France and England had not repaid the United States for the loans made to them in the form of war materials and supplies such as airplanes, ships and guns. The United States demanded that the Allies, France and England, repay every cent of borrowed money they were given during and after the war.

The United States was lending money to Germany in order for them to pay for war reparations to the Allies, who in turn could repay the United States. That policy was self-defeating; for the U.S. was lending money to Germany then Germany was passing the same money to the Allies. The Allies then were passing the same money back to the United States to pay war debts. Nothing was being gained. In addition to this nonsense-lending, the United States passed laws allowing Germany to pay back loans over a longer period of time, which slowed the ability of the Allies to repay their war loans and by the end of the 1920s, very little had been repaid. Once the Depression began, there was little hope that the loans would ever be repaid. In fact they were not repaid until 1957.

Some thought the economy was improving when the war had ended two years before in 1918. Some of the leaders of the country thought society was stable. A closer look at what was happening told a very different story. The population of the country was restless and agitated. There was a mixture of immigrants coming from all over Europe of all colors, religions, and languages.

After the turn of the 20th century, there was a mass immigration from Europe and western Asia to the United States. German, Italian, and Polish people came to America in great numbers looking for a better life. They wanted jobs and a place where they could have freedom of expression and they could own their own homes.

They were good, steady workers who were willing and able to prove their worth to any employer. They worked in every type of industry. They were coal miners, farmers, steel mill workers, stone masons and merchants.

The immigrants were a welcome source of labor. They were truly needed as the country tooled up to provide war materials, food and manufactured products for the Allies during World War I. By the end of the War, when the economy slowed, they had established themselves and their families in homes that were paid for and they had become substantial members of their communities.

In the early years of their migration from the "mother country" they tended to live in communities of their own ethnic groups, which gave them the support of the people who helped them get started when they first arrived in the United States. It was through the support of their fellow countrymen that these immigrants were able to survive during the troublesome years of the Great Depression.

Overall, the country only had 50% of inhabitants that were native born. The years of the 1920s were a time of the "haves and have-nots". Half of the total work force of the country was engaged in agriculture, while the remaining half was engaged in manufacturing. In the mid-1920s, when prices of farm products dropped below the cost of production, many farm families moved to the cities thus creating over-crowding and increases to the unemployed population.

The "haves" were saying everything was all right and the stock market was in good hands, but this was not true. Wealthy owners of stocks and bonds continued to invest their surplus cash in the market, while credit was over-extended to those with limited ability to pay. Stock profits and dividends went way up. The apparent health of the economy was very misleading. The 1920s were far from being a prosperous time for our society as many of the wealthy who benefited from these times implied.

As early as 1925, speculations were being made that the country's economy was not in good condition. There were many who did not believe the economy was in trouble because investors in the 1925 Florida land boom and other ventures were reaping huge profits. The New York Federal Reserve Bank cut its discount rate which made it much easier for borrowers to obtain funds for one-time purchases and the volume of trade increased through most of 1928. Fortunes were made and lost in the same day. Businesses put all of their profits in the Market and they encouraged their employees to do likewise. The commencement of buying on time caused corporate sales to show a dramatic increase. With a high return on stocks and bonds being sold, there was a frenzy of activity. Property would be sold one day for a large profit and the same property would be sold again the next day for another high profit. This activity in the market was acting more like a huge Ponzi scheme rather than a legitimate business operation. Many people who were making large profits every day couldn't possibly imagine that such activity would end. When the market failed they were the ones who suffered the greatest losses.

The good times in sales could not continue for the market at home had been glutted and the overseas markets had dried up. This fact did not stop the manufacturers from continuing to produce goods and stockpiling them in warehouses hoping the market would change. Real prices for goods and the consumption of goods fell due to low wages and periods of high unemployment. As the economy worsened high pressure sales tactics were being used in order to sell more goods, which led to more and more goods being purchased on the time payment plan with little or no down payment. Much of the sales on the time payments were to low paid employees with poor credit. Very few of the citizens in 1928 and early 1929 had any idea that the economy of the country was about to collapse. When the market did collapse in October of 1929 nearly everyone was taken by surprise. The Great Depression of the 1930s cannot be attributed completely to the fall of the stock market. A sudden change from easy credit to a condition of severe credit restrictions had a major effect on the nation's economy. President Herbert Hoover said at the time of the market failure that the Depression would be over in just a few weeks. He felt there was no reason for the government to step in and give aid for voluntary aid would provide what was needed and the worst would be over in no time.

The worst days of the Great Depression were the years of 1932 and 1933. Relief did not begin until the election of President Roosevelt. When the he took office he immediately set government programs in place to provide jobs and money for the unemployed and money for the hungry homeless people to buy food. It was the beginning of a recovery that would not be over until the country was plunged into war with Japan in 1941.

This was the era of the "flapper", young good-time ladies who had access to the good things in life. Those with wealth flaunted it by spending time in the dance halls and cocktail lounges. They were the carefree lot that owned or controlled most of the men who had most of the money. Automobiles were becoming a regular mode of transportation and those with money could buy cars, radios and the latest fashions in clothing. The flapper era was a time of booze, and parties for the wealthy. Although the prohibition law was passed in 1920, it did not mean there were no alcoholic drinks available. The law gave rise to the manufacture of moonshine, home-brew, bathtub gin and other forms of illegal beverages. Bootlegging became a way of life for many and rum runners brought in alcohol from Canada and from Cuba by boat. This illegal activity provided an opportunity for the Mob who gained control of much of the illegal whiskey operation.

Most of the population thought that World War I was a pointless war. General opinion was that the United States should never enter into a war unless the homeland was threatened. The idea was it was Europe's war, let them fight it. American society was in the middle of some important transitions. It was no longer quite so rural in nature but not yet dominated by industry. The interest of people at that time in the elections was very low. In the 1920s spectator sports began to really boom. Organized football and baseball games, and boxing matches were popular, and those who could not attend listened to the games on the radio. Movies also began to be popular and available during this period which gave rise to many famous movie stars. These were years of hero worship which included movie stars, foreign dignitaries, famous murderers, bank robbers and Charles Lindbergh. Henry Ford was considered a man of great achievement for his development of the Model T Ford. The growth of the automobile industry caused Congress to pass the Federal Highway Act to provide roads for the increasing number of cars. Automobiles were using nearly all of the nation's petroleum products, 80% of the rubber and 25% of the steel. Henry Ford's factories turned out a new Model T Ford every four minutes in the 1920s. Every other car on the road was a Model T Ford.

Manufacturers were turning out goods but there was no market for the products overseas. The market at home had already been saturated and the goods were piling up in warehouses. The economy in the U.S. was slowly coming to a halt, workers were being laid off and plants were closing. Things became worse in 1926, 1927, 1928 and then in October of 1929 the stock market crashed. Things were bad enough, but they were to get worse. The entire economy of the U.S. was practically shut down. It was devastating for those who had money in the market and only served to worsen things for those without investments.

After the collapse of the stock market things continued to worsen until 1932 when all the banks failed and people lost everything they had deposited. There were many who had no money in the banks nor did they have funds in the market yet both of these failures affected them directly. Small businesses and farmers couldn't get loans to furnish their needs to make a living. The subsistence farmers had a difficult time producing enough of a crop to pay their mortgage, taxes and fertilizer bill. At the time, there was no government help for farmers and it was not until late in 1935 that the government gave them any help at all. The price of cotton, corn and tobacco had fallen to a point where they were no longer profitable crops. Many small farmers were losing their land to the mortgage holders because they could not make the payments. The Great Depression continued almost unabated through the 1930s until the war got under way in Europe in 1939. Orders started to come in to the U.S.to provide war materiel, and food supplies to the Allies. Factories were retooling to make the war goods, employees were called back to work and the stalemated economy started to function once more. This was only the beginning, for the U.S. government had no desire to enter the war in Europe by providing troops, though the government did wish to be prepared if war was forced upon the country.

In January, 1940, a military draft was started to call up young men to be trained for service, just in case. The draftees were to be trained for two years. Then they would be discharged and remain in the Army reserve. It was a fortunate move because Japan bombed Pearl Harbor in 1941, forcing the United States into war just days before those early draftees were to be discharged. In addition to the draftees, there were three million CCC (Civilian Conservation Corps) workers available for service. They had been placed in a work force starting in the mid-1930s to provide employment and build national parks. They were trained in camps just like soldiers. These men were ready and trained to enter the service and they did so when Pearl Harbor was bombed.

Were it not for the war in Europe and the war with Japan, the Depression may have endured for another 20 years.

Chapter Four

The Will Smith Family

The Smith family home was old but it was well built of logs that had been finished on the inside with boards and batten strips. All the cracks had been sealed with clay to keep out the cold winter winds. The roof was covered with corrugated sheet iron and the outside walls were covered with board and batten.

Will Smith's family had lived on their 80 acre farm for three generations raising corn, tobacco, cotton, potatoes, hay for their cows and horses and a large kitchen garden to feed the family during the growing season. The garden supplied enough so that the extra produce could be canned and put up for the long winter months when nothing would grow in the garden except collards, kale and turnips. Apple, peach and pear trees would provide enough dried fruit to last until the following season. It would take a good crop year to provide enough for their growing family of seven children.

The eighth addition to the family arrived the last week in March and it was a girl child. Soon after the birth, the baby showed signs of hunger. Her mother moved her to a full breast and the child began to feed. She was to be the last of the line of Smith children.

Will Smith fished in the river when the seasons and the weather were not fit for farming. There was always a market during the Depression years for crossties that were used by the railroads to support the iron rails along the tracks. A good off-season job from which farmers could pick up a few dollars, was cutting and delivering crossties to the station agents of the local railroad. There was plenty of timber on the local public lands that could be obtained just for the taking. The timber from hardwoods and pine trees was suitable for the making of crossties.

A two man crew with a crosscut saw and axes could cut, saw, square and finish six crossties per day. Each crosstie was worth $1.25, delivered to the nearest railroad station master. After the ties were made, a two-man crew would carry one crosstie at a time out of the woods to the nearest road. When a dozen ties had been finished and carried to the nearest roadway, they would bring their horse and wagon and haul the ties to the railroad station. It would take the two men three days to cut, finish and haul out twelve ties. For the three days work they would receive $15.00 for the two of them or $7.50each which was good pay for the Depression years. $2.50 per day was considered very good pay for the average laborer was only getting 75 cents per day.

In addition to cutting crossties, there was always a job cutting logs for the local saw mill which also paid 75 cents per day. Another job available at times was cutting and hauling firewood for heating and cooking. These jobs were infrequent and didn't pay very much.

In mid-April of 1921, there came up a freezing rain. Will had gone out early that morning to the river with the fishing crew and before the day was over he was soaked through with cold rain. By the time he arrived home from the river he was running a high fever. Next morning he was unable to get out of bed because he had come down with pneumonia, double pneumonia. The fever was still raging and nothing seemed to abate it. The doctor came early that morning but he was unable to help for in those days there were no antibiotics to cure pneumonia and the usual cures did little or nothing to break the fever. It was only a matter of time. On the third day he became delirious and on the morning of the fourth day he passed into the next world.

Matilda Smith, known to her kin and neighbors as Tilley, was now a widow with eight children to feed and look after with one of the children less than a month old. The two older boys were fourteen and fifteen but they were old enough to work in the field and they could also care for the horses, cows and hogs. The two older girls could work in the fields with their older brothers. They helped in the fields when the worms were to be picked from the tobacco leaves and picked cotton when it was ready. The three younger girls would be mother's helpers at the house and look after the baby girl.

Tilley was able to make it even though it was difficult. Their home was a sound log house with a good roof, heated by a big fireplace and a cast iron cook stove in the kitchen. The 80 acres of land were owned free and clear. There was a smokehouse and it was full of good smoked ham, bacon and sausage enough to last until hog-killing time in November. As soon as the weather moderated and spring arrived the boys could seed the tobacco bed. After the tobacco plants were started for the new season, the corn field would be plowed and the corn planted as soon as the frost was over. Tobacco seedlings would be set out in early June. The spring kitchen garden would be plowed and planted with beans, peas, turnips, kale, carrots, mustard, potatoes, radishes and pumpkins. The older boys and girls would be busy all summer taking care of the crops and the garden and Tilley was there to help with all of it and guide them.

When the children's work was caught up for a few days they would work for their neighbors to earn a bit of cash. Field workers could make 50 cents a day. Work of this sort would provide money for the items they needed that could not be raised on the farm. It would be an uphill battle but with all the family working they could make it. The early years in the 1920s were rather chaotic. The price of farm products was way down. Corn, cotton, tobacco and grain prices were down so low the farmers could hardly make enough to pay for the seed and fertilizer. Railroads laid off employees and many of the banks were going under due to bad mortgage loans. Many of the property owners were unable to pay the taxes on their holdings and they were losing their homes and their lands due to foreclosures.

By the mid-1920s, things got worse in the national and world economy. There were no overseas markets for goods manufactured in the United States. Factories were closing their doors and going out of business. In 1929 it all came to an end. The stock market closed its doors and thousands lost their life savings. Banks started closing and depositors lost everything. Jobs were not available anywhere in the country. It was a miserable time for everyone. Men were riding the trains as hobos going from one place to another seeking any kind of work they could find just to be able to feed their families.

These were very serious times but what everyone did not know was that times were to become harder yet, for the Depression had only begun. The 1930s turned out to be much worse than the previous decade and lasted for the next 10 years. As soon as Franklin D. Roosevelt took office as the new President, he started the WPA (Works Progress Administration), a government funded program that provided work for many. The Civilian Conservation Corps was another government program that was started in the mid '30s. This program made work for young men by providing jobs to develop new parks and recreation areas throughout the country. These programs were not the complete answer to the problems of the country but they did provide for the basic needs of the families that had nothing. To make matters worse, the weather turned bad in the mid-west and dust storms ruined many of the farmlands causing the displacement of the entire population of the area. Tilley Smith had managed to eke out a living for her and the children. She had fallen behind in paying taxes on her land after the stock market crash but the county had been lenient, allowing her to pay what she could and thus delay foreclosure. The county could be lenient for just so long, then they would be forced to foreclose. It was with this in mind that Tilley had thoughts of acquiring another husband to help out with the expenses that were piling up and to have another farm-hand to help with the work. Working the farm and tending to the needs of the children was a full time job, an almost impossible task for one woman even with the help of the boys.

She knew of a suitable prospect that might be able to help. He was a member of a respectable family that lived on the west side of the county. His name was Sam House his family was involved in business at the state capitol and he was a veteran of World War I having served with the Expeditionary Forces in France in 1917 and '18. He had never married. He was a vain sort of ass but he had money and had shown interest in the widow Smith and her children.

For Tilley and the family it could be a good partnership and she might be wise to pursue with diligence the prospect of improving her lot. All summer he would bring his buggy and fancy trotter horse over, pick her up and take her to church. She would have dinner fixed before going to church and after dinner, they would spend the remainder of the day on the cool front porch in friendly conversation.

Early in the fall of the year, they were wed and he moved in and became a part of the family. Very soon after the marriage it was found that he would not work. Farm work was beneath his dignity. He preferred to groom his fancy trotter horse, saddle her up, put on his riding breeches, boots, and ten gallon hat and with his riding crop in hand, go off to visit friends or spend the day in town.

The end of the year was tax time and he was approached about paying up the taxes but this was not agreeable to him without certain commitments being made. If he were to pay the taxes then he must be made a partner in the ownership of the land. Or he must be given a lien on the property in the amount of taxes to be paid and a suitable rate of interest to be paid on the debt at regular intervals until the amount of the taxes and interest had been paid.

A few days had passed without Tilley's agreement to his demands for paying the taxes, so he came up with another scheme which she might accept and a plan that would reward him handsomely. The new proposal was that Tilley would sign the farm property over to himself and her eldest son making them the new joint owners. He would see to it that the taxes were paid up to date and that they would be paid every year from then on. Tilley was not that amenable to the new proposal.

After she had discussed the situation with her eldest son, who was to be the joint owner of the property, she acquiesced. She agreed to sign over the property to the two of them as joint owners with the provision they would each prepare a Last Will and Testament that was irrevocable and was registered at the county courthouse. The will must state that in case they die before Tilley, the ownership of the property would revert back to her.

Tilley knew now that she had made her bed of nettles and she would have to sleep in it, so to speak. She knew that her son would never sell his portion of the property regardless of what Sam had in mind. Now that Sam had the property he became more arrogant and even less productive around the place. All he wanted was to be provided each day with food of his choice and be able to travel around the county on his horse and do as he pleased.

He was never quite satisfied with anything around the house and when he disliked the food he would throw it across the room, plate and all. After the second episode of this behavior the two older boys got up from the table and each of them grabbed an arm and threw him to the floor. They told him if he ever did that again they would kill him. In addition, they forced him to pick up the broken plate and clean the floor. It stopped the food throwing but then he commenced to pick on the younger children. He would call them names, criticize everything they did and berate them until they were in tears.

Since Sam now had a controlling interest in the property, he felt he could do as he wished as long as he didn't cross the two older boys. He was not really too concerned about Henry causing him trouble for

22

he was the oldest and the partner in the land. He thought he would be able to control him.

His trips on his horse into town and around the county became more frequent and he only returned home for his meals and his sleeping quarters. The children all developed a hatred for him, avoiding him whenever possible. What had Tilley done? She had swapped the misery of loneliness and lack of funds for the devil, however suave and debonair Sam had seemed at the outset of their relationship.

It now looked as if she had traded her soul for a "dish of porridge". She came to the conclusion that she would find a way to tolerate this asinine fool but in the meantime she was sure that the taxes would be paid and that she and the children would have a home as long as she lived.

Little did Tilley know at the time but fate was to take a hand in the near future concerning the ownership of her property. Sam had taken to riding more often and many times he would race his horse at full speed just to show off. He would race through the thickets that surrounded the farm by following the cow paths and rocky trails through the countryside. It seemed to be Sam's way of proving his skill and horsemanship to himself. He knew deep down that he was the best but so far no one else had noticed or given him credit. If he practiced every day with his horse he was sure to become the best in any horse race around the county. Pearl Harbor had just been bombed and the war with Japan had commenced. A horse race was planned for the following Saturday and several of the local horsemen planned to enter the race, including Sam. The race would prove who the best horseman was and who had the fastest horse. It would show his erstwhile friends how fast his horse could run over rough ground and through the woods. The race had just begun when Sam's horse stepped in a hole on the path and stumbled. Sam left the saddle headfirst, striking his head on a large boulder on the side of the trail. By the time help arrived he had departed this life.

After the funeral, his will was probated and now Tilley was half owner in her property and she was once more a widow. Sam left her

23

more than just the property for he had not made a specific will for the remainder of his estate. Since there was a will for the property, the judge ruled that she was also entitled, as his legal wife, to the remainder of his estate. Sam was not a rich man but he did have considerable funds in the bank, other investments and an insurance policy. Now Tilley would have enough to pay the taxes, maintain the property and see to the well-being of the younger children. Maybe her gamble to obtain some security had paid off after all.

Tilley still had two young girls at home. The rest of the children were either in the military service or married or otherwise making their own way in the world. She and the two girls who were at home would not be able to farm the land, so she decided it would be best to let it out to share-croppers.

Maybe the local banker could suggest someone who would be interested in farming the land on halves. then she could have a substantial income from the farm. If a share-cropper could not be found then maybe she could rent the land. This would have to be looked into. After several inquiries she found that one of the local farmers would rent the farm land for $50.00 per month, providing her with cash flow that would help pay the bills.

During the war years everything was rationed. Butter, sugar, gasoline, tires and many other things but most of these things were not needed by the family. They had no car so they didn't need gasoline or tires. They didn't need butter, either. They had plenty, for they only had to milk the cows and operate the churn. Sugar was made from molasses crystals and syrup from the sugar cane would provide the molasses. Steak was also in short supply but they had their own supply of beef and pork. During the war years, they would have plenty of corn meal but wheat flour would have to come from rationing. The family made out all right in spite of the rationing.

When the war was finally over items were no longer rationed but many were still in scarce supply. New automobiles were not available from one to two years depending on the models. During the war years, there were fifteen million men and women in the armed forces. When they all came back to the States, they needed everything from houses to automobiles. Houses were being built by the thousands and still there were not enough for every veteran who wanted one.

Many of the veterans wanted to take advantage of the G.I. Bill provision that the government made available to pay for tuition at college. The colleges and universities were overwhelmed with applications for student entry. Many veterans were turned away because there was no room for them in the schools.

The wartime factories closed when orders for war materials ceased and some retooled to make peace-time goods. It was difficult for most veterans to find work after they were discharged from the service. Many of them did not reenlist and they needed jobs.

In 1938, Henry, the oldest Smith son was accepted into the Civilian Conservation Corps program. The government was training young men to be foresters, park workers, bridge builders and road builders. Henry's assignment was in north and the winter weather was very severe. He was able to stick it out and each month his mother received some money from his salary.

In 1937 Hitler invaded the Sudeten land in the Alsace Loraine area. The Nazi army was poised to take over any area that was taken from Germany after the close of World War I and in any other place in Europe they wished to conquer. In 1939 the big push of the German army moved into Poland with a blitzkrieg that destroyed the country in a very short time. Next the German army moved into the Netherlands and northern France creating a real threat that England would be the next country to fall to the Nazi might.

In the United States in 1940, the government began the national draft of all young men and training programs were begun for these new military recruits. The President and Congress felt that the country should be prepared just in case the war came to the United States. Each young man was to serve for two years and then be discharged. None of the draftees were able to be discharged, for Pearl Harbor was bombed on 7 December 1941. These draftees were the first of the combat troops that were moved out to the Pacific area at the start of the war with Japan.

Henry Smith became a member of an infantry regiment as part of the 6th Army. Their first engagement with the Japanese was at Buna on the southeast coast of Papua, New Guinea. An Australian infantry division was moving over the Owen Stanley Mountains from Port Moresby, General MacArthur's headquarters, to attack the Japanese forces from the land. The American 6th Army moved up the coast of New Guinea by boat and landed on the beaches at Buna. It was a tough battle and Henry's outfit lost a third of their men while making the beachhead landing.

From Buna, the 6th Army moved into Lae, the next town north of Buna, where the fighting was intense but Henry's infantry regiment was making progress in removing the enemy forces. The men of the regiment were suffering from malaria and from dengue fever which was caused by the mites in the kunai grass that covered the whole area near the beaches. Henry was sidelined by these ailments to the field hospital in Finschafen, after his unit secured Lae. Then the regiment moved out over the Finistere Mountains moving northwest pushing the Japanese ahead of them. Their objective was the capture of the large Japanese naval base at Madang. The enemy was cleared from Madang, the area secured and the regiment prepared for their next big objective: the seaport of Hollandia, and the gateway to the Japanese Sentani Airbase. By that time, Henry had recuperated and rejoined his regiment. After the Hollandia area was secured, the 6th Army including Henry's regiment got a brief respite but they were soon slated for another major battle.

Their next encounter with the enemy would occur at Biak Island, a major Japanese air base and a strategic location for air support for the invasion of the Philippine Islands and MacArthur's promise to the Philippine people that he would return. A beachhead assault operation would be on 6 June 1944 the very same day of the invasion of Germany and the landings on the coast of Normandy. Neither of the forces knew what the other was doing until it had been done. Henry's infantry regiment was in the thick of the fight starting with the first day of the landing. The landing force came under heavy mortar and artillery fire from the first day of the operation. As the infantry moved into the island on their way to secure the airstrip at Mokmer Airdrome, they were constantly coming under fire from enemy gun positions hidden in the many caves that covered the island. The fighting was so intense the troops were not able to secure the airstrip until the seventh day of the operation. As soon as the island had been secured the 6th Army prepared for the invasion of the Philippine Islands and would spear-head the landing at Tacloban.

The Japanese forces were well entrenched in the Philippines and the first landing of American troops on any of the islands would be met with considerable resistance. In addition to the ground force resistance, there was a Japanese naval buildup in the area and the 6th was not only bombarded by land-based artillery but also received fire from guns on the enemy ships off shore. It was here on his first military operation in the Philippines that Henry received a Purple Heart Medal, which is given for wounds received by direct action of enemy fire. He spent two weeks in the field hospital for a bullet wound in the lower part of his right leg and fortunately there were no broken bones. Henry's next movement would be the amphibious assault landing at Lingayen Gulf, an area north of Manila, and Clark Field. The purpose of this engagement was to establish a foothold on the main Philippine Island of Luzon, move south, capture Clark Field, then move south to Manila and secure the harbor and the island of Corregidor.

After the 6th Army and Henry's regiment landed at Lingayen Gulf, they moved inland with the infantry regiment at the point. One group would move north to relieve the prisoner of war camp that the Japanese had established for the retention of the Death March prisoners when Corregidor fell to the Japanese in 1942. Another group, Henry's company, would move south and east to meet up with a group of Philippine guerillas who had maintained a running fight with the Japanese since the occupation of the island had begun. Henry was now a platoon sergeant and his platoon was at the point when they came under heavy enemy fire from across a small river. He called for mortar and artillery fire to cover the area which quieted down some of the enemy fire but there was still an enemy machine gun on the far

27

side of the river that was preventing further progress. Two of Henry's point men had been wounded as they approached the river. They had to be rescued. The two remaining point men were moved to where they could bring fire on the machine gun position and cover Henry while he crawled forward to rescue the wounded men, one at a time. On the first try he was able to reach the first man and drag him to safety but he was wounded in one leg and an arm. On the second try he was able to reach the remaining wounded man and bring him to safety but he was shot again, this time in the other leg plus a flesh wound to his hip. The three of them were evacuated to the field hospital on the beach. It was there that Henry earned his second Purple Heart and, in addition, he was awarded a Silver Star Medal for exceptional heroism in risking his own life to save the lives of two of his men.

While Henry and his two fellow soldiers were in the field hospital, news came that an atomic bomb had been dropped on Hiroshima, Japan. Two days later another atomic bomb was dropped on the Japanese city of Nagasaki. It was only a few days until Japan agreed to a cease-fire, ending the war. Henry and the wounded men were transferred to a hospital ship and sent back to the States for further medical treatment at the Veterans Hospital in Nashville.

After recuperation Henry was assigned to an Army Reserve Unit stationed at Fort McClelland. It was there that the Commanding General held a Post parade. The General decorated Henry with the Silver Star Medal. He then invited him to join him and his staff in the review of the troops and accept the salutes of his fellow soldiers. Henry's mother, Tilley, was invited to the decoration ceremony and she stood with the invited guests. That day she was so very proud of her eldest son. He was truly her hero. After the ceremony, Henry was given a 60-day R & R (rest and recuperation) leave and he went home with his mother.

After his leave was up, Henry made the decision to remain on active duty, with the thought of maybe staying in the service for twenty years and retiring. There were not many jobs available for the returning war veterans. Thousands were coming home every day

28

looking to get out of the service, find a job and settle down. Since he was now a decorated Master Sergeant, the pay was good and the peace-time army should be easy. His first choice for an assignment was overseas in Europe. There was a need for occupation troops there and this need would continue for some time in order to assure that the peace was being kept. When he returned to camp he requested assignment overseas in the occupation forces to be stationed in Germany. Since there was a great need for experienced troops there, his request was granted, and orders were cut for him to report to Camp Kilmer, New Jersey, for immediate shipment to Europe. Within ten days he was on the old U.S.S. George Washington troopship headed across the Atlantic Ocean. His destination was Bremerhaven, Germany. As the troopship entered the English Channel on a bright sunny morning, the white cliffs of Dover, England, could be seen in the distance shining as if they were mirrors.

Upon landing at Bremerhaven, the troops were processed for assignments, put on trains, and shipped out to their new areas. Henry was now the First Sergeant of a detached special construction company stationed at Giessen, in an old German army camp located forty miles north of Frankfort am Main on the Autobahn. The company's job was building a hospital at Grafenwöhr, where a new Army training camp was being built. Henry's main jobs were overseeing the personnel, maintaining the barracks, keeping daily communications with regimental headquarters in Russelsheim, and keeping a record of all the daily activities and work schedules.

Henry was amazed at the destruction of the cities and towns in Germany. His brother, John, had fought during the war in Germany, and had told him of the conditions there but he was not prepared for the sights he met with upon his arrival. Bombed-out buildings lay where they had fallen. They had never been cleaned up. People were living in basements where the buildings had been blown apart. Food was very scarce for the German people. There was no dependable source of meat or other foods. The farmers had potatoes and some wheat for flour but little of anything else. Those were indeed hard times for the Germans. Later in the year of 1946, the Red Cross was able to commence providing some food and supplies. By autumn, the Marshall Plan began to supply some of the needs of the people.

His four year enlistment was completed, and he returned to the States in May of 1950. He had not completely decided whether or not to stay in the service. But one thing he did want to do was to marry his high school sweetheart. She had waited all these years for him. They were married on the 15th of May and while they were on their honeymoon war broke out in Korea. All active duty military personnel were recalled. He received orders the next day. The orders read, "Report to Seattle, Washington, no civilian clothes, no automobile, no dependents. Be prepared for immediate shipment overseas". The orders came as a tremendous shock, for he had no idea that he would be called upon again to fight another war in such a short time. Of course, the politicians in Washington didn't refer to this operation as a war. It was politically referred to as a "police action" but those who were to fight in Korea, knew quite well it was indeed a war, one of the bloodiest yet.

The infantry battalion that Henry was assigned to was made up of mostly World War II veterans who had stayed in the service and wanted to make a career of the army. He was assigned to the heavy weapons company that supplied the mortar and machine gun fire to support the front line as the troops engaged the enemy. No one knew really how long this "police action" would last. It was not only a fight between North Korea and South Korea. Other nations had become involved. Red China was providing thousands of infantry troops to support the North Koreans. Russia was providing guns, ammunitions and combat aircraft. It was shaping up to be a nasty war, same as all the other wars. A strategic area would be taken one day and lost the next, to be fought over, time after time. "Pork Chop Hill" was won and lost so many times no one knew how it could be secured for good. As winter approached, the weather became another enemy. During the cold months, it was extremely difficult for the troops to operate in the field. Army field equipment was not made to keep troops warm in such severe winters as they experienced in Korea.

That war provided an opportunity for Henry to add to his collection of medals. His management of the heavy weapons section won him a Bronze Star for his service above and beyond the call of duty. He had rallied his men to stay with their weapons while they were being overrun by a horde of Red Chinese infantry. He acquired another Purple Heart Medal, when he again caught a rifle bullet in his right leg, which sent him to the Army hospital in Japan.

After he had surgery on his leg and the bone was reset he was shipped home. At the Army hospital in Nashville, he spent four months recuperating. His new assignment would be another tour of overseas duty and this time it would be in Japan. Here his wife could come over and be with him on this tour. At the military base near Atsugi, he would be an instructor for new recruits coming for duty in the area. When his wife arrived, they were assigned to a military housing project near the base. For the first time this was good duty, the best any soldier could expect. After his four year enlistment was up, he decided to reenlist for four years at the same station and then retire back to the States. With twenty one years in the military service, he and his wife and their two children moved back to the old home place to take care of his mother, Tilley, who was up in age and was having problems with her heart, plus rheumatism. She needed someone to take care of her the rest of her years. Henry and his wife were the answer for he was half owner with his mother of the property and she was glad to have the two young grandchildren in the house. Being back at the old home place was good for Henry. He had plans to develop a herd of Black Angus beef cattle. The farm would provide plenty of good pasture and enough hay could be cut from the fields to provide forage during the winter months. His first herd was ten cows. These were bred the first year and they brought him ten calves the following spring. Each year he would buy five more cows. With new calves coming every spring, he was accumulating a nice herd. After the first year on the farm, he commenced to purchase the farm equipment that was needed to cut hay, bundle it and move it to the barn. The old barn had to have major repairs and a new larger barn was needed and was built the second year. In addition to the repairs on the barn, he had made repairs to the house, as it had not had any maintenance during the war years.

When the herd reached forty head of mature cows, Henry decided that was as many cows as the farm could support. As the calves came in each year, he would sell them at the cattle auction. The income from these sales would provide money for fertilize, winter feed supplement, and maintenance of the farm equipment. Since the old home had not been modernized, he and his wife decided they would start a savings account especially ear-marked for a new home. There was a beautiful location out nearer the county road and the house could be built under the shade of two large oaks. With the regular sale of calves, it would soon be possible to start building. By their fourth year in the cattle business, they had saved enough money to start their new home.

In the summer of 1943, the second Smith son John was drafted and he was sent to Camp Edwards, Massachusetts, for training in anti-aircraft warfare. These troops learned to operate the half-track vehicles that were mounted with four 50-caliber machine guns and they learned to fire the guns for anti-aircraft protection from enemy planes. John's battalion spent the fall and winter of 1943, training in New England. Early in the spring of 1944 the battalion boarded a troop transport and sailed for England. They were one of the first units to land on Omaha Beach the morning of 6 June 1944.

The landing was terrible. There were obstacles on the beach everywhere. Machine gun fire was coming from the many German gun positions along the cliffs. The battalion managed to get to the beach and secure a safe position with the loss of only seven men and three half-track tanks. This unit would be the anti-aircraft protection for the 14th Armored Battalion of Sherman tanks.

As soon as the troops were ashore, they moved out with Patton's Third Infantry Division, through the hedgerows of Normandy. The first days ashore were frightening and dangerous. There were German troops everywhere and each small French town was a trap for the incoming Allied soldiers. German tanks set up roadblocks at every intersection, machine guns were hidden in the hedgerows alongside the roadways, and all the bridges across the streams were demolished by the retreating Germans.

Saint Lo, a French town located on the road to Paris, was surrounded by the Allied troops for three days, but the Germans occupying it would not give up. The town was finally taken after it had been completely destroyed by bombs and artillery. After much hard fighting, the troops finally reached Paris on their way north to Germany. But there was bitter fighting yet ahead. Each town that was encountered had to be blasted to the ground before they could move on through to the next objective. Winter was almost on them and the Battle of the Bulge would be the greatest challenge for the men of Patton's Third Army.

The German army had broken through the Allied lines and was throwing all of their armored and infantry might at the Allied lines that were approaching the German border. It was Hitler's last ditch effort to destroy the Allied forces and prevent them from entering the German mainland. John's battalion was caught in the forefront of the German movement and for three days they were behind the German lines. Each day there was the possibility that they would be found and captured but they were finally able to break out and rejoin the main body of Patton's troops.

When the Battle of the Bulge was over, John's unit moved out and crossed the Rhine River near Mainz, Germany. That took them through the German fortified area of the Siegfried Line. The Germans had built a line of underground gun positions along the north side of the Rhine River after World War I to counter the Maginot Line, a series of French fortifications along the south bank. The half-track battalion was now attached to the 17th Armored Division and they moved along the north side of the Rhine River to Karlsruhe, then on to Munich. When the war was over the unit was almost to Austria.

Participating in the Hammelberg Raid was one of the highlights of John's service in Europe; in fact it almost got him killed behind the German lines. There was a German prisoner of war camp for captured officers of the Allied armies located in Hammelberg, a small town 30 miles inside the German lines. This was in the area where the Russians were poised to push through and capture the town. The local Army commander was concerned as to what the Russians might do with the American and Allied prisoners that the Germans were holding in the camp. In fact it was rumored that the American Commander's son-in-law was being held there. Tanks from the 17th Armored and the half-track anti-artillery units were chosen for the job of relieving the camp and bringing out the prisoners. The task force was going well. They had reached the camp without being detected, broke through the camp gates, overpowered the guards and proceeded to load the prisoners into the tanks and half-tracks. They were discovered by German tanks positioned in the area near the camp just as they were leaving with the prisoners. The Germans fired on the fleeing units causing many casualties, and putting several of the American units out of action.

On the way to the camp, the Americans had crossed a bridge over a small river. In the meantime, the Germans had destroyed the bridge so the tanks could not cross back over. Some of the half-tracks managed to bypass the bridge area and continue but most of the tanks were left behind. John's half-track managed to make it safely back to his unit with most of the crew and wounded prisoners that had come with them. This effort won John two medals. A Purple Heart, and a Bronze Star for extraordinary courage in performing a difficult task in the face of heavy enemy fire on the return trip with the prisoners. Only a few of the original task force units and a few of the released prisoners made it back to safety.

The war would soon be over in Europe and some of the units were being prepared to ship back to the States. From there, they would go to the Pacific Theater to help finish that war with Japan. But this was not to be the case with John's unit. It would stay in Germany, be moved to Mannheim and become a part of the occupation forces. John's unit took over the Military Police duties for the area. They were in charge of all the security and would control the movements of all transportation in the area and in general be the local police force. One day while John was on patrol with two other motorcycle-mounted military police, they were called to the scene of an accident. A truck had run into a jeep and there were casualties. They arrived at the scene, and recognized that it was a General's jeep and driver. Both had been seriously hurt in the accident. They called an ambulance and got them to the hospital. The General died the next day of his injuries. John's unit stayed on in the occupation force until March of 1946, when they were shipped back to the States.

John took his discharge from the Army and signed up for his G.I. Bill of Rights education benefits. This enabled him to be admitted as a freshman at the University of Tennessee. He spent four years in college and received his bachelor's degree. While at the University, he was also enrolled in the Naval Reserve Officers Training Corps. At graduation, he received his commission as an Ensign in the Navy. It was in June 1950, that he graduated, near the time the war was starting in Korea. Rather than be called to service in the Army, he opted to go on active duty with the United States Coast Guard Service in his new capacity as an ensign.

Before he entered service, John and his high school sweetheart, Pauline, were married. She was able to join him at his first assignment in Mississippi. After the first year at Biloxi, his unit was transferred to Alaska, and she joined him there, also. There were quarters for married couples on the post. After a four year tour of duty in Alaska, his unit was transferred to Hawaii for the next four years of duty. By this time, their family included three children. It was the best tour of duty they had ever had and they would have stayed there for another tour but that would not be the case. After Hawaii, his unit was moved to the Coast Guard Station on Lake Erie. This was the station where he expected to remain until he retired. However, this did not happen. While stationed there, John was promoted to Commander in the Coast Guard. His duties now were in the Coast Guard Headquarters. His superior officer was a young lady with the rank of Captain and he reported directly to her. At times it was necessary for the two of them to travel to Washington to report the activities and participate in the planning for the office. Many times these trips required them to spend a week away from home.

The young Captain was quite beautiful. She was a graduate of the Coast Guard Academy, and had a perfect record of service. She was also single. An officer with her credentials could expect to be promoted to Admiral in the future, if she continued to perform well. John was promoted to the position of her Executive Officer. This meant the two of them spent considerable time together in conference, planning the operation of the Station. On many occasions John had to work late in the evening and many weekends. Trips away from the Station became more frequent for the two of them.

There were no dependents' quarters on the Station. Each family was given quarters allowance so they could find their own home. John and Pauline had rented a nice home west of town where other members of the Station also lived. The school for the children was nearby and the military commissary was only two miles away. This area was very handy for the dependents. All the services they needed were close at hand.

With John away from home so much and the children in school all day, Pauline found time to go to school to qualify as a Licensed Practical Nurse. The training she received was to come in handy in the near future. Things were not good at home. John was not there very often anymore and when he was there, he and Pauline were always at each other about one thing or another. She was commencing to realize that John had other interests which were more important to him than his wife and family.

It was not very long before he broke the news to Pauline that he wanted a divorce. This came as no surprise to her for she had suspected something was going on at the office. There were rumors from some of the other members at the Station concerning the activities of her husband and the Captain and the amount of time they spent in traveling. Pauline agreed to the divorce, for she had become fond of one of the doctors at the hospital where she trained. She went to work in the hospital as a LPN and within three months she was married to the doctor she had worked with. Fate stepped in and the doctor died nine months later, leaving Pauline a widow.

36

Pauline continued to work at the hospital after the demise of her husband. It was a good place to work, the salary was good and it kept her busy ever day of the work week. Weekends were spent with the two children that were still at home. The older boy was in the military service. He had joined the Air Force. The two girls would soon graduate from high school. One would go to the local college and the other would follow her brother's footsteps and join the military. Early the next year, Phil Bass, an old friend from Pauline's home town dropped by to see her. The two of them had gone to school together. He would be working in Cleveland for a while until his project was completed, in about three months. It was a good diversion for Pauline since the kids were all on their own now. She would have someone to go out with in the evenings and on weekends. Phil's wife had passed away two years before and he was footloose and free, with an idea of remarrying. This suited Pauline and within the next two months they were married and on their honeymoon in Florida.

The Captain at the Station was transferred to the Coast Guard Station in Miami. She managed to get John transferred to the same station. The two of them were married within the next three months.

When Sarah, the eldest Smith girl, graduated from high school in 1939, she went for a visit with her Aunt Celia, who had no children and lived in Birmingham, Alabama, with her husband Robert Manis. She was welcomed with open arms. Her aunt always wanted a daughter but never had one. Now she asked Tilley if Sarah could live with her and her husband, to help out around the house for they were getting up in years. Sarah's mother gave permission for her to live with her aunt and uncle. She thought it was a good idea. Sarah was happy with the idea of living with her aunt because she wanted to get away from Sam and his constant harassing of the girls. She also wanted to be living in a big city. This was something new to her after living in the country all of her life. There were also many opportunities for a young person to get a job.

Aunt Celia's husband worked for the telephone company and it wasn't very long before an opening for a telephone operator became available. Sarah applied for the job and was hired. She made a good salary and was able to save most of her earnings. After she paid her room and board at her aunt's house and sent some money home to her mother to help out, she had money left over each payday to start a savings account. Now she could plan for her future and the possibility of marrying. She hoped she could meet a good man and someday have a family.

Sarah continued to live with her aunt and uncle throughout the war years working at the phone company and saving her money. She didn't have much opportunity to meet young men of her age since they were nearly all in the service and only women worked at the phone company. After the war was over and automobiles became available she bought a car so she could go visit her mother when she had time off from work. As her aunt and uncle grew older they planned to leave their home and their estate to Sarah when they passed away since they had no children or any close relatives that needed a home.

Her uncle retired from the telephone company in the late 1940s as his health was beginning to fail. By this time he had in his thirty years of service. He passed away in the early 1950s and after his death Sarah cared for her aunt until her demise in the late 1950s. Now she was the owner of the home and the entire estate of her aunt and uncle. She was a wealthy young woman, just turned forty years of age and had been promoted to supervisor work. Another ten years with the telephone company and she could retire with a pension that would nearly equal her regular salary. She had not completely forgotten about finding a good man and getting married but had become a very low priority. Now she was concentrating on the remainder of her career, planning visits with her mother on weekends, and looking forward to relaxing and enjoying life.

When it became time for her to retire, she planned to travel, see some of the United States and then maybe go to Europe and take in some of the sights of the old world. She could tour Europe, going by boat to England, then to Holland. She could travel the Rhine River by tour boat to Basel, Switzerland. While in Switzerland, she planned to go to Interlaken and travel up the cog rail line to the Jung Frau to view the snow-covered tops of the Alps. A visit to Bern would be entertaining, as well as a beautiful encounter. Going south through Austria to Salzburg, she could visit the home of Mozart and attend the summer Mozart Festival, then on to Rome, Italy. From Rome, she would board a plane for home.

When she retired, she did take her dream trip to Europe. On the ship going over she met a traveling companion, a man who was also planning to do the tour. He was older than Sarah, a fine looking man, well-mannered and mature. They were dining companions at the Captain's table on the first two evenings at sea. After dinner he asked Sarah if she would care to join him in the ballroom where they could dance to the music of the band.

Sarah accepted his invitation for she had always dreamed of meeting a gentleman of this sort and dancing away the evenings. Maybe this would truly fulfill her dream. The evening passed quickly as they danced every dance. He was a wonderful dancer and she enjoyed every minute of it. When the dance was over, he saw her to her stateroom door. Again the next evening they dined at the Captain's table and after dinner they retired to the dance floor. This gentleman's name was Robert Anders, a retired stock broker from Atlanta who was widowed two years before. He and his wife had one son who was married and lived in New York. Now that Robert was retired, he wanted to travel. This was his first venture out to see the remainder of the world. It was lonely living by himself in his big home overlooking the Chattahoochee River. This whirlwind romantic encounter seemed too good to be true. Sarah never gave a thought to checking into the matter further or getting more information concerning Robert and his intentions.

Sarah and Robert enjoyed the entire tour together. By the time they returned to the States, they had gotten to know each other quite well. They discussed the possibility of seeing each other after they returned home. A week after they were home, Sarah received a phone call from Robert saying he would be in Birmingham the following week on a business trip. He dropped by and invited her out for dinner.

She said yes and he had a surprise for her. After dinner he asked her to marry him and come to live in Atlanta. Sarah was not really surprised for she thought maybe he would ask her to marry him. She said yes. She would lease her home in Birmingham and move to Atlanta to live in Robert's house on the river. By leasing her home it would bring in some revenue and she would always have a home if things didn't work out in the future.

Robert's house in Atlanta was located near Roswell, where a small dam had been built years before. This was a favorite fishing spot for trout. Robert often fished the river in the evenings by standing on the dam and casting upstream. It was one of his favorite pastimes. As Sarah was to find out later on this was not his only pastime.

During the first six month of their marriage, they had a wonderful time as there was much to do and enjoy around Atlanta. There were ball games of one sort or the other most all the time. The Fox Theater was always having special events for theater goers and dinners at the posh clubs downtown were a true delight. Shopping at the many malls around the city was very rewarding with a large selection of merchandise of all types, available. Sarah was thinking that Atlanta could be a fun place to live.

Before the end of the first year, Robert was required to go downtown at frequent intervals to take care of some business. Usually he stayed until after dinner and sometimes later. At first this seemed normal and Sarah had no concern about the business appointments. As the trips downtown became routine, and the fact that they lasted sometimes into the wee hours of the morning started making her concerned and suspicious that something besides business might be taking place. She soon learned that Robert was having an affair with an old friend, Henrietta Wilkes, a lady he had worked with in the past. She was the owner of an employment agency with an office downtown in Atlanta.

After a few discreet phone calls to some of Robert's friends, she discovered that his evening trips were not all business. According to some of the informants, this had been going on with Robert and Henrietta even before his first wife, Susan had passed away. Friends of his first wife informed Sarah that she knew of the affair but she chose to ignore it and do her own thing and let him do his. She was not happy with the situation but she didn't wish to leave him. There were other things she could amuse herself with while he was out having his fun.

Susan belonged to a group of friends that spent a great deal of time in the night clubs and bars around town. They would meet for lunch on Friday where "two-fors" were being served. They would remain there for dinner and more drinks after dinner. Robert never liked the idea but many times he was not home when Susan arrived there late at night, anyway.

It was these parties and late-night drinking bouts that caused Susan's death. She and her friends made it a practice to meet at different "watering holes" every weekend. Sometimes, they would be east of the city in DeKalb County, and then out in Cobb County near Marietta and other times they met downtown in Atlanta. One night during a snowstorm when the roads were iced over Susan was returning home, "three sheets to the wind" and driving fast. She hit the iced-over bridge on the Chattahoochee River. Her BMW spun out and struck the bridge railing, flipped and fell into the river. By the time the rescue crew arrived the car had drifted downriver a quarter mile. Her body was still in the car when it was finally dragged from the icy water.

Sarah was reluctant to confront Robert with the fact that she knew what he was doing and who he was seeing on his business trips. She would wait until he was ready to tell her and if he didn't, she would then make her move. She didn't have to wait very long before the problem was solved, not by her, but by the powers that be. Sarah was not about to turn to the bottle as Susan had done.

Robert spent a few evenings a week fishing from the dam in the river. It was his habit to put on his waders, get his fishing gear and walk out on the dam and fish the backwater. The constant moisture on the dam caused moss to grow on the surface and it became very slick when wet. As he was fishing one evening after dark, his foot slipped and he fell into the river. No one saw the accident but they found his

41

body the next day downriver three miles away. Now, there was the problem of settling Robert's estate After their marriage, he had made a new will giving Sarah a half interest in his estate, with the other half going to his only son. The will was probated after the son arrived in town. Sarah was allowed to live in the home until the estate was settled.

After the settlement Sarah returned to her home in Birmingham. She was so glad she had not sold her home. When the lease had been terminated, she settled back in her home and contemplated what she would do with the rest of her life. Another marriage would be out of the question, for this first encounter with marriage was enough to last a lifetime.

Maybe this would be a good time to get in touch with some of her siblings for she had heard that Beth was there in Birmingham. It seemed a good idea to try to contact her if she could. She had never agreed with Beth and her lifestyle but then she had the right to do whatever she wished with her life and Sarah accepted that. After several attempts, she found Beth's address and phone number and called her, inviting her to lunch on Saturday. It was a great surprise for Beth and she was happy to be invited to Sarah's home. This could be a great reunion of two sisters who had spent too many years apart. The lunch was a wonderful time for both the sisters. They spent the full afternoon and evening telling stories of their lives while they were apart for the past twenty years. It was an interesting visit and they planned to see each other again soon. Over time the two sisters became close again and spent a great deal of time together. On one visit Sarah wanted to know why Beth had decided to leave home and spend so much time away. Beth had no reason not to tell Sarah the whole story of how she came to choose the life she had lived for the last twenty years. It was obvious to Sarah that something must have happened to cause Beth to leave home and stay away for so long.

Sarah knew there was a problem between Beth and Sam soon after he married their mother but she had no idea it had become so serious. Sam was always making rude remarks towards the girls when he was out of earshot of their mother and the two boys. They tried to ignore his actions but he continued to irritate them.

Sam would call the girls whores when they would put on makeup. He would say they should wash their faces and get that powder and rouge off. Anytime they went anywhere he questioned them continuously trying to find out who they were with and what they did while they were out. Even when they were at church, he wanted to know which boys they talked to and what was said. Sam became so obnoxious the girls would avoid him every chance they got. Tilley could not do anything to stop Sam for most of his tirades took place when Tilley was not around. It was the older of the girls who received most of his criticism.

Beth's chore was to do the milking and one evening while she was at the barn working, in walked Sam. He commenced to make crude remarks to Beth and began to suggest that they could get to know each other better in the hay barn. His behavior infuriated Beth and she waited for her chance to solve the problem once and for all. She had taken all of Sam's abusive treatment that she intended to put up with. Now was the time to do something about it. As Sam approached her, she drew his attention away from her by suggesting that he move the feed barrel for her. As Sam turned away from her for a moment to move the barrel, she grabbed his right arm and twisted it up behind his back. As she put pressure on his arm, she told him if he ever suggested that they have a sexual encounter in the hay or if he ever approached her improperly again, she would kill him. If she couldn't kill him, she would tell her two older brothers and they would do the job very gladly. As she twisted Sam's arm, she had pushed him down on the floor of the stable and slammed her knee into the small of his back. With his arm twisted out of joint at the shoulder and Beth's knee in his back, he could not move and the pain was terrible. He didn't scream or holler but he did listen closely. He was told not to mention this encounter to anyone. If they asked what happened to his arm he was to tell them he slipped and fell. She gave the arm one more jerk before she let him up. She finished her milking and took the milk into the house. Sam got up and went to the house holding his disjointed arm with the good hand. When Tilley saw him, she wanted to know what in the world happened to him. He told her the story that he fell. She got hot water and liniment and bathed the arm and finally worked it back in place but it was a painful process. When the arm had been treated she made a sling to support the arm. He would have to wear the arm in a sling for a week before he could use it again. Every time Beth looked at him after that he would turn away knowing he would like to get even with her. He was afraid to do anything for he knew that if she didn't do him in she would tell the boys and they would delight in teaching him a lesson he would never forget. After the food throwing incident earlier, he had grown to respect Beth's two older brothers for they had no love for him anyway. After the encounter in the milking barn, Beth decided it would be best that she get out on her own. She knew if she remained at home sooner or later she would have to take matters into her own hands and teach Sam the lesson she had promised him that evening. By this time, Beth had become tired of the life in the country where there was little to interest a young woman of her age. She longed to see the rest of the world and to have a chance to make her own way.

Sarah was appalled with the story that Beth had told for she had no idea how far Sam had taken his harassment of the girls. She knew from the start when Sam joined the household that he irritated all of the girls even the youngest girl Leatha. After the food throwing deal, he commenced to aggravate all of the girls. It seemed a means to get even with the boys for threatening him. Sam was not a great threat to Sarah for she moved out of the house to live with her aunt and uncle as soon as she graduated from high school. She really didn't know the extent of Sam's irritation of the other girls. Sarah and Beth soon became very close and since Sarah had the big house all paid for she agreed for Beth to move in with her. They could share the household duties and they would be company for each other.

Rebecca (Becky) was the next oldest girl in the Smith family. She was one of the prettiest and smartest of the girls around. After graduating from high school, she was able to get a job as a secretary at

Camp Shelby. Her boss was a young Lieutenant who was the assistant Post Engineer. His name was Joe Ellis. She was only nineteen but she was good at what she was doing. Most secretaries couldn't make decisions, handle telephone inquiries or prepare correspondence on their own but Becky had the ability to handle all such matters with or without the help of the Lieutenant. If her boss goofed off and wanted to be out of the office and away from the phone so he could not be contacted by the Colonel, she could handle the problem. Some secretaries would tattle to the Colonel that the lieutenant was on his way to the Club or some other such place, but not Becky.

The Officers Club on the Post was an interesting place for all the single officers, especially. Every weekend there was a Saturday evening dinner dance and on Sunday there was always a tea dance. Becky had heard of these affairs and she wanted very much to attend and to see how the officers lived. At times she would casually mention to the Lieutenant that she sure would like to go to the Club and to one of the dances. He seemed reluctant at first to get involved with an employee, which could lead to problems in the future. However after a few more hints concerning a visit to the Club dances, he relented and asked her for a date on Saturday. Joe had come to realize how much he would love to walk into the Club with this beautiful doll on his arm and see the envy in the eyes of the other bachelor officers.

They arrived early and were one of the first couples on the dance floor. He could see now that this would be a wonderful evening for Becky was an excellent dancer. On each of the tables there were dishes of appetizers such as popcorn and peanuts. The usual dinner was served: rib eye steak, green peas, potatoes au gratin, green salad and a butterscotch pudding for dessert. After dinner, dancing resumed and as was the practice the lights were turned down low for personal reasons because sometimes officers would attend the dances with a lady other than their wife.

At times, some of the older ladies with low-cut gowns displaying ample cleavage would leave the dance floor abruptly and head for the ladies room. It seemed strange that several of the older women were leaving the dance floor about the times Joe and Becky were dancing in their vicinity. After the dance, on the way home, Becky could not keep it a secret any longer. She had to tell. As she would leave the table, in her right hand she would get a few kernels of popcorn and from behind Joe's back, she could very deftly flip a kernel into one of the ladies' low-cut dresses. In the subdued light, no one knew from where the popcorn came. She was so proud of her secret accomplishments that she just had to tell someone. To Joe, this was not funny. If she had been apprehended doing such a trick, the two of them would be barred from the Club and Joe would have been reprimanded for bringing such a trickster to the dance. After that, when they were at the Club and they started for the dance floor, Joe would inspect both of her hands to see that they did not contain popcorn or anything else that could be used as a small missile.

Becky Smith was fond of practical jokes. Once when Joe had his feet up on his desk and was on the phone, she slipped into his office and grabbed his shoes. She knew that the Post Commander and the Colonel were due to visit the office and Joe was scheduled to escort them on a warehouse tour within the hour. She took his shoes and left the office. He got off the phone and couldn't find his shoes. Since he didn't have time to get more shoes before the inspection, he decided he would just go on the tour in his stocking feet.

The inspecting officers arrived on time and as Joe stepped out from behind the desk, the Colonel noticed that he was barefooted and asked about his shoes. All he could say was that someone had stolen his shoes and that he had not had time to replace them before their arrival. The Colonel brought out a pair of shoes that he had hidden behind his back and asked him to do the "Cinderella Trick". That is, if they fit he could have them. Sure they fit. They were his shoes. The Colonel had found them on the steps outside the office. Joe was reprimanded for being so careless in leaving his shoes on the steps. He was sure that Becky had put the shoes there, then called the Colonel and told him where they were and to whom they belonged. It was a good thing that she had left the office by the time the inspection was completed for she had committed the greatest of military sins. She had embarrassed a young "shave-tail" in the presence of his superior officers. Such a sin was intolerable.

She was full of tricks and she delighted in doing them. It soon became time for Joe to go on overseas duty to Germany. Becky saw him off at the train station and they promised to write and stay in touch. Two years passed quickly and Joe came home. Becky was waiting for him when he arrived. They picked up where they had left off a couple of years ago. It seemed that nothing had changed but somehow there was feeling that all was not what it once was and that there was something that had not been said.

Joe was stationed in Washington and when he got leave six months later he came home and went directly to see Becky for he intended to ask her to marry him. She met him at the train station and they caught up on old times. At two thirty she told Joe she had to run for she was getting married in Meridian, Mississippi, at six that evening. She asked if he would drive up with her and attend the wedding for it was to be a small affair at the home of the groom's aunt.

Sure, he would go. The bride was entitled to something old, something new and something blue. He was all three wrapped up in one package. They arrived at the aunt's house early and the groom, the clergyman, and the other guest had not arrived. It was a good time for the two of them to slip out on the sun porch and say their last goodbyes before the ceremony. There was a close embrace and a long kiss and Joe had lost the beautiful "Kewpie Doll" that he thought he had won at the fair.

Her husband was a young Ensign in the Navy, by the name of Harry Oakes. He was taking flying lessons at the training center in Texas. He had just completed his primary training. His next training would be in California, in fighter planes. After another year of training he was ready for active service overseas. He graduated and received his wings in May 1950, the month before the start of war in Korea. Orders were received for his fighter unit to report to Seattle, Washington, for immediate shipment to Japan.

Becky was not happy. She and her husband had not had much time together since their marriage, because of all his military duties and the training. Now, he was going overseas. She decided to go back to her old job at the base if it was still available and settle down until Harry could come home.

The fighter plane unit moved into South Korea and began to engage the MIGs that the Russians were flying in support of the North Koreans. It was dangerous fighting. The pilots had never had any experience against the Russian MIGs. It was a learning process to figure the maneuvers these foreign fighter planes were capable of and how the pilots would react in combat. Many American fighter planes were lost in the early engagements with the enemy.

Harry wrote to Becky as often as he could and she stayed in touch by writing a long letter every week. Then came the bad time, for she received notice from the government that Harry was missing in action and was presumed dead. This came as a terrible shock for Becky. How would she ever know for sure what happened? Would the military continue to search for him? Finally she received word that he was shot down behind the enemy lines. His wing man saw the plane get hit and followed it down until it crashed. His personal effects were gathered up and mailed to her.

Becky was in a state of shock for weeks after she was notified of Harry's demise but she knew deep down that such a thing might happen in wartime. In a few weeks she managed to write Joe a long letter telling him of the loss of Harry and how he had been shot down behind the lines. When Joe received the letter he planned to go to see Becky on his leave the following month. Their visit was a good one. They spent time together remembering the early days when she worked for him. They relived the fun things they did in the times past and it brought the two of them closer than they had ever been. The visit helped Becky to relieve some of the stress of her recent loss and allayed her fears for the future. Now she could go on with her life and maybe she and Joe could take up where they left off some years ago.

Joe spent his entire ten-day leave at the base where Becky was working. He was able to get one of the guest quarters at the Officers Club so he would be nearby. They spent their evenings together at the Club, having dinner and dancing every dance to the jukebox tunes. On the last weekend, they attended the dinner dance at the Club on Saturday and the tea dance on Sunday. The weekend brought back old memories of several years past when there was popcorn to be thrown into the ample cleavages of the older matrons attending the dances. But now that Becky was older and more mature, there was no danger of such a thing happening now. The few days on leave passed so quickly and it was time for Joe to return to his station at Fort Belvoir, Virginia. Becky saw him off on the train and they promised to write each other and stay in touch.

On the train trip back to his base, Joe thought the situation over and made up his mind that he would ask Becky to marry him. He would call her and ask her just as soon as he returned to Fort Belvoir. If she said yes, they could be married in the Base Chapel and the reception could be held at the Officers Club located on the banks of the Potomac River, just south of George Washington's home, Mount Vernon.

He called, and asked if she would marry him on the Post and she said yes! Could she take leave of her job and come right away so the wedding could be planned? If so, she could stay in the Guest Quarters until the wedding. Afterward, they could live at Fort Belvoir because married Captains were entitled to have quarters on the Post. One week later, Becky arrived and the wedding preparations began. The wife of Joe's Commanding Officer volunteered to take charge and help with all the planning and the arrangements for the Chapel Service.

Within two weeks, all the details for the wedding and the reception were in place. The wedding ceremony would be on Saturday afternoon at 1500 hours and the reception would follow at the Officers Club. The invitation had been posted on the bulletin board at the Club and all the officers and wives of the Post were invited. After the normal Saturday night dinner the regularly scheduled dinner dance would commence. These dinner dances were provided by the Senior Commanding Officers assigned to the Post.

There was a long-standing tradition at the Club whereby a real effort was put forth to separate a bride and groom for the first night of their marriage. It was supposed to be fun and if the newlyweds were not aware of the tradition it was, of course, a great, though unwelcome surprise. Joe knew about it for he had participated in several wedding receptions at the Club in the past. He informed Becky and they were prepared for the attempts to separate them. As the party was getting into full swing and the drinks had been flowing quite freely he and Becky slipped out the patio door near the pool and disappeared before anyone missed them. It was just a few steps to the parking lot and they were in Joe's car and on their way to the Hotel in Washington, to spend their honeymoon night.

On their five-day honeymoon, they traveled to New York and spent a day and night seeing the sights, and then visited Niagara Falls. They returned to the Post and settled in their quarters in the officers housing area. It was a very nice, quiet area, close to the Club, and away from the daily activities of the Base. At the weekly social gatherings at the Club, Becky became acquainted with most of the ladies of the Post. It was a wonderful experience for her to participate and to become a part of the women's activities.

Joe was the Adjutant of the Transient Officers School Section. This was the section where officers from all over the States came for special training and refresher courses. Most courses lasted for three months and then another group would arrive to attend classes. These student officers were billeted in barracks in the "L" Area, which included their officers Mess Hall and their recreation building. These officers were not members of the Post Officers Club. The area was close enough that Joe could be home with Becky every day for lunch and it was a nice situation for both of them.

On the weekends the two of them would go sightseeing in Washington D.C. There was a visit to the White House, and to the Washington Monument with a climb up the steps to get an aerial view of the city. They visited the Capital where there was a chance to meet their congressman from home. One whole day was spent visiting the National Cemetery, seeing the many war memorials and a visit to the Unknown Soldiers monument. The Smithsonian museums were a real treat for both of them for there were so many wonderful things to see and experience. On a nice day they would go to the National Zoo to walk around the in the beautiful surroundings and view the wonderful, exotic animals.

Before their first year was finished, it became time for Joe to be deployed overseas. This time it would be to Salzburg, Austria. He would be the Headquarters Commandant of a Special Engineer Construction Battalion that would build a new military base for the housing of the occupation troops. The Battalion would supervise Austrian contractors in the erection of the buildings and installation of utilities. Battalion troops would do the construction of the roads, hardstands and special installation items. It was an interesting assignment and a worthwhile experience for all of the troops.

Becky was to join him just as soon as he could locate suitable housing in Salzburg. There was no military housing available but there were Austrian houses that could be rented. Joe was able to find a new chalet on the east side of town with a beautiful view of the sunrise over the Austrian Alps. Becky was flown over with a group of military wives two months after the unit had arrived in Salzburg. Joe located an automobile that was for sale and purchased it so Becky would have transportation to shop at the military commissary and run errands around town when needed. Their furniture arrived before Becky did, so it was set up and their home was ready when she got to Salzburg. It was the better of two worlds for now Joe could be home every night unless there was a special reason to remain on Base.

Now that they had an automobile they could take trips around the area to see the sights. A trip to Berchtesgaden was just a short drive away and there were so many interesting things to see. Visiting one of the wood carving shops was fascinating. One shop had nothing but cuckoo clocks of every size and type. There were other shops that sold only glass figurines. Before their tour of duty was over they were able to visit Switzerland and most of Austria. They even visited Vienna and saw all the famous sights. When Joe's tour of duty was completed they returned to the States and Joe was discharged from the service. They settled in their new home just outside of Meridian. Joe used his G.I. Bill credits to return to college. He needed one more year to get his degree in Civil Engineering. When he graduated he got a job as a Highway Engineer for the State.

Beth was the next oldest girl and she graduated from high school just at the beginning of the war. In high school she was a cheerleader and was on a first name basis with all the school athletes. She was very popular with the boys. Her goal in life at this time, after graduating from high school, was to begin a vigorous pursuit of the opposite sex, that being boys. She had no desire to get married and settle down or get involved in having children who would tie her down. Circumstance and fate are apt to join forces and create unwanted situations at times and so they did for Beth. She had seen how women had learned to be free and independent.

In 1920, Congress passed an amendment to the Constitution that allowed women to vote in elections for the first time in the history of the country. Jazz music became very popular and the women were dancing the "Charleston" in the public dance halls. Short skirts became the vogue in young ladies' dresses and now it was all right for women to do as they pleased.

During the years of World War II, young women had joined the military and worked in the aircraft factories. Women were no longer relegated to being housekeepers, cooks and stay-at-home wives. Beth didn't want to bother with these mundane things for she was young, beautiful and had a burning desire to set the world on fire one young man at a time. There were so many young men and each of them reacted differently to her sweet female charms. Soon she had perfected her approach to conquest. She became cocky, self-assured and pompous. The pigeons were hers to pluck, feather by feather. What a feeling of exhilaration and satisfaction! She had arrived and her goal had been attained at the tender age of nineteen. Now it was time for her to move out and make a place for herself in the world.

Sooner than she had expected she met her Waterloo. Willie was a young man, slightly built, who wore horn-rimmed glasses. He was an "egghead" type and the son of a local cotton farmer. This young man had not been drafted yet but he could be called up any time now.

She and her family had been invited to Willie's father's farm for a Labor Day picnic and barbecue. The year's cotton crop had been picked and stored in the cotton barn located a quarter of a mile down the road from the house. In due course, Beth was setting the stage for her next sexual encounter. Her mind had been made up long before she arrived at the farm that Willie would be her choice of the day. It had been rumored that he was a virgin. If indeed it was true then this could be a real challenge.

The evening continued, the barbecue was served and everyone had eaten. Then she set the trap. While Willie and Beth sat close on the bench under the big umbrella chinaberry tree, she quietly mentioned that she would like to walk down to the barns to look at the horses. She even suggested if it was not too late they might saddle up and go for a short ride down the pasture lane. He warmed to her suggestion and they slipped away quietly to the barns, holding hands as they hurried along. They spent a few minutes in the horse barns close to each other, she pressing her firm breasts against his back. Now was the time for her to suggest they check the cotton barn to see how much cotton had been picked. As they walked rapidly to the cotton barn with their arms around each other it became evident to Beth that this time she would score for sure and this time, with a virgin.

As the two of them entered the barn, the door shut gently behind them. She seemed to trip and fall sprawling into the huge pile of soft, fluffy cotton, pulling Willie down beside her. They rolled and tumbled in the soft piles of cotton. In the rough and tumble play her halter became unfastened and Willie was pulled close against her warm full breasts and they lay there wrapped in each other's arms. At that crucial moment they heard the hired man call out, "Willie is that you in there? I just wanted to let you know I will be putting the cows in the stalls for milking." Willie jumped to his feet leaving Beth to put on her halter and straighten her hair. Not a word was said as they left the barn through the back door to a path through the field that led to the house. She had failed and he was still a virgin.

This first failure was to weigh on her mind and would be in her thoughts for some time. Occasionally, in odd moments and sleepless nights, she would pause to reflect on the failure of this evening. What went wrong? Why hadn't she known of the hired man and his milking schedule? She knew in her heart if there had not been an interruption from the hired man her mission would have been accomplished and Willie would no longer have been a virgin. He had been responding so naturally to her fondling and coercion, he would certainly have responded favorably to her wishes.

Beth's brother, John, was in the Army and stationed at Camp Edwards, Massachusetts in an anti-aircraft artillery unit. Now she learned that Willie had been drafted and assigned to the same unit as her brother. She thought it would be wonderful if she could go visit her brother for a week or so for he was scheduled to be shipped out soon. While she was there at camp she would get a chance to renew her acquaintance with Willie if she was fortunate.

John would send her money to come and she could have a room in the guest house at the service club for a week. It would be a wonderful adventure. When she arrived at camp John and Willie were there to meet her and show her to her room at the guest house. It was a wonderful week. She enjoyed every minute of it and there were so many young men at the club in the evenings. There was a dance scheduled every Saturday and Sunday evening and there were always plenty of dance partners. She spent much of her time with Willie. John informed her that his unit was shipping out and she would have to go home after the following weekend.

The last Saturday in camp, she had decided that she would have Willie propose marriage to her and she would accept. Could she pull this one off? Sure she could, if she put her mind to it. The two of them went in to Providence and while they were there they were married. Now Willie could know that he had a wife waiting for him when the war was over and he came home. In the meantime, Beth could be getting an allotment check from her husband's Army salary. In addition, she saw to it that Willie made her the beneficiary of his

$10,000 government life insurance policy just in case any thing happened to him.

Beth went back home after John and Willie shipped out. Now came dull times for her. The crops were ready to be worked and everyone was needed. The garden needed attention. Weeds had to be pulled from the vegetable rows, cabbage plants had to be set and watered, beans had to be picked. There was plenty of work for everyone in the household. Beth had made up her mind there had to be a better way. She didn't want to be a farmhand all her life. She had been home now for a month and it was almost the end of June.

Every day she checked the mail as soon as the carrier arrived at their place. She was looking for a letter from Willie or John, maybe from both of them. Instead she received a letter from the U.S. Government. The letter informed her that her husband Willie had been killed on Omaha Beach on D-Day at Normandy, during the invasion landing. It also informed her that she was to receive his $10,000 government insurance money and the check would be in the mail to her very soon. This was both bad news and good news. Now she had no husband but she did have funds to do with as she pleased.

While she was home, one of her old high school boyfriends, Tom, came home from camp on leave. He was stationed on the Gulf Coast. He dropped by to see Beth and it was old times all over again. The two of them were together for the entire week of his leave. When it came time for him to return to camp, he suggested she come there to visit him. As soon as he returned to camp he would find her a room or small apartment nearby where they could be together when he could get a pass to be off the Post.

Within a week of his return, Tom had procured a small efficiency apartment at Sopchoppy, Florida, the small town near the camp and had written for her to come on down. She was on her way as soon as she received his letter. Upon arrival at the apartment, Beth settled in and then went into town to find a part time job to help with expenses. Of course she had money from the government insurance but she planned to save that and live on what she could earn during the week and what Tom Weeks, her lover would be able to provide.

Tom was a Master Sergeant and he visited the apartment most every weekend that he didn't have special duty at camp. Her job as a waitress at a local café only required that she work Monday through Friday so she had the weekends free to be with Tom. There was plenty of entertainment. The U.S.O. club was located in the town and there was dancing there every weekend. The beautiful Gulf of Mexico beaches with white sand and blue surf were near and available for swimming. But paradise never lasted very long in the Army during the war years and after three months Tom's unit was scheduled to move to the west coast. The unit would move to Fort Ord for further training prior to shipment overseas to the war front in the Pacific.

Beth and Tom agreed that she would move out to California so she would be there when the troops arrived. This would allow time for her to find a place to live and a job. Monterrey, a small town on the bay, was located three miles from the Post and there was a large sardine cannery there. An apartment was found and the cannery needed all the help they could get. Beth was able to get a job the first day and the pay was good. Now when Tom arrived they had a place for the weekends. There was also a beautiful new U.S.O. Club on the post at Fort Ord and there were dances and music every weekend and the Club was open seven days a week. It proved to be a perfect place for lovers to get together and spend their spare time.

Time was drawing near for Tom's unit to depart for overseas and Beth had to give some serious thought as to what she would do after Tom was gone. Maybe it would be the smart thing to convince Tom that they should be married before he departed. After a week or so she was able to persuade him to marry her as soon as possible. They went into Monterrey the next day and were married, with a reception held at the U.S.O. Club on the Post. Tom took his furlough and the two of them spent the week in San Francisco and had a wonderful time. While on their honeymoon, Beth convinced Tom that he should make her the beneficiary of his government insurance policy, just in case anything would happen to him and he did not make it back from the war.

Two weeks later Tom's unit had moved up to Camp Stoneman, located on the Sacramento River forty miles northeast of San Francisco. They would remain there training and being oriented to overseas duty for a period of three weeks. Beth chose to follow Tom to Camp Stoneman. She arrived ahead of the troops and found a small apartment where she could stay. Now she had a place for Tom when he could get leave from Camp and they could enjoy as much time as they could before he left for overseas.

All too soon Tom's unit loaded aboard a river boat at midnight on a very rainy and cold night and shipped down river to Fort Mason. There they boarded a troop transport for the Philippine Islands. When the amphibious assault task force departed Manila Harbor, Tom's artillery unit was part of the operation, which was the invasion of Okinawa, the last big push before the invasion of the Japanese homeland. The first two days of the operation were terrible and the fighting by the Japanese was fierce. One of the regiments lost over 60% of its men in two days. Tom's artillery unit did not reach the beach until late the second day of the operation. They managed to get ashore and set up their guns with the loss of only a dozen men and three of their artillery pieces. Their unit was under constant enemy artillery and mortar fire for the first week they were ashore and it had been impossible to move forward. They stayed dug in at their first day position for seven days before they could move closer to the fighting front. On the eighth day of the operation the unit moved closer to the front so they could bring artillery fire to bear on the caves where the enemy guns were hidden.

The first night after the move the artillery unit was attacked by a "banzai" charge. A group of fifty Japanese infantry troops broke through the defense perimeter by throwing themselves on the barbed concertina wire to make a bridge across. The guards were overcome, the perimeter machine gun crews were killed and the enemy soldiers moved in and shot up the gun crews as they lay in their foxholes near the guns. When daylight came and the charge was over there were eleven men of Tom's unit lying dead, including Tom, who had led the defense of the gun positions. Of the Japanese soldiers, there were thirty nine dead, lying scattered over the area. None of the big guns had been destroyed. It was obviously the aim of the banzai to destroy the artillery pieces.

When Beth moved up to Camp Stoneman and found an apartment she also found a job as a waitress in a barroom in Pittsburg. This would help out with expenses until her allotment came through which Tom had made to his wife before he left for overseas. In due time, Beth was notified of the death of her husband and that the $10,000 government life insurance funds would be forthcoming.

She would remain in Pittsburg for the time being until she received her money from the government and then she would decide what to do in the future. As soon as everything was settled she decided to return to the old home area and settle somewhere near Birmingham, after all she had kin in the area and her older sister lived there. At age thirty seven she was slowing down in her pursuit of worldly pleasures and so she would find a small home, a job and settle down to the good life. After all she had money enough to purchase a small home, and with a job she could have an automobile and travel when she wished. This would be the start of a better way for Beth. After all the war should be over soon and maybe later on she would be able to meet a good man and settle down.

With some effort in searching the area around Birmingham she was able to find a small home at the end of the street car line on the west side of town. The price of the home was such that she could qualify for a G.I. loan on the basis that she was the widow of a war veteran. She could make the mortgage payments even before she found work. She moved in and set up house-keeping, managed to get enough furniture to provide for some comfort and now for once in her life she felt she could stay in place for a while.

For the next few days she made applications for employment and with her status as a war widow she was able to find work quickly. The war was not over yet and there was still a shortage of workers. She was hired at Dove's department store as a clerk in the ladies hosiery department. She worked six days each week. Hours of employment were from nine in the morning to eight at night. It made a long work day but it suited her needs perfectly. She would not have time on her hands to reflect on the past or worry about the future. Maybe she would look up her sister who lived in Birmingham and maybe she would accept her as "the lost sheep that had been found." She would not have to wait very long before her sister, Sarah, would look for her and take her in as her long lost sibling. The two of them would spend the remainder of their days together in the big house that Sarah had inherited from their aunt and uncle.

Margaret was the next oldest girl in the family and she was known to all the family and close acquaintances as Maggie. Maggie was a loner. She did things her way. At sixteen, in her second year in high school, she ran away with Jason Harris, an older member of the community and they went to Nashville to live. He was a good looking, ne'er-do-well, who loved to dance and party. There was no way he was going to keep a steady job for after partying all night he would not show up for work and he would get fired. It took a while then to find another job and frequently it was temporary. He would just work a few days or be on call if they needed someone. He worked sometimes and sometimes he just loafed. Since Jason could not be depended upon to make a living for them, Maggie had to go to work as a maid in one of the local hotels. There were no children for she didn't want to be a stay-at-home mother.

She also loved to party the same as Jason but she realized that one or both of them had to provide for the fun and games and that meant they had to work and bring home a salary to pay the bills. For five years she put up with Jason's nonsense and his lack of help in providing for the two of them. It was just too much for her to support them both in the style they had become accustomed to and working in the hotel as a maid was getting old. She wanted a change. She divorced Jason and moved out.

Just before the end of the war, a kitchen appliance manufacturer needed employees in their plant. Maggie applied for and was accepted as one of the appliance assembly persons. It was a good job, the pay was good and the working hours were excellent. Soon she was able to save some money, something she had never before been able to do. Jason had spent what they both could bring in and was never satisfied even with that. It was best she was rid of him. On Saturday evenings she would frequent the local tavern for dinner, a couple of drinks and a dance or two with the local single customers. Many of the workers from the appliance plant hung out there on the weekends and it was good to be with some of her fellow workers. One evening she met a young man by the name of Wiley Comer who worked in the sales department. He was single and at the tavern by himself. He joined her at her table and the two of them had a drink together and then they danced. He was a wonderful dancer and they spent the evening getting acquainted. They decided this could be a good thing for both of them and they agreed to see more of each other.

Wiley was too young to be in the service during World War II but he wanted to serve since his older brother was overseas during the war. When he graduated from high school the war was almost over but he did enlist in the army and wanted to serve overseas. Since the war had ended by the time he completed basic training there was no need for additional combat troops overseas. Wiley was assigned to a special unit where he trained as a Military Police. He never served in combat in his four years in the service. By the time he had finished his enlistment the factories were in full production making consumer goods to fill the needs of the war years. It was at that time he was able to get a job in the sales department of the appliance plant. Now that he was gainfully employed he had money to party with and funds to buy a new car. He could enjoy more of his new-found freedom. On the weekends, he spent time visiting the local entertainment spot and this is where he met Maggie.

During the next three months they saw a great deal of each other. They would meet on the weekends at the tavern for dinner, drinks and dancing, and it became a routine thing. Sometimes they would meet, have dinner at one of the local cafes and then go to a drive-in movie. Wiley had a new Chevrolet convertible coupe and it was such funs to go to the drive-in, let the top down on the coupe, open a cold beer and enjoy the movie. Many times they would party most of the night on Saturday night.

It was only a few more months before they decided to get married. They went to the courthouse and made application for a marriage license. The following weekend they went across the state line into Kentucky to see one of Wiley's old friends who happened to be a notary public and allowed to perform marriages.

While they were there at the friend's house that Saturday, they mentioned that they were to be married and that they had already made application for the marriage license in Tennessee. The friend suggested that if they wished he would marry them while they were there that day. The question was brought up whether it would be all right since they had made application for license in another state. The notary assured them that it would be fine so they proceeded with the ceremony and the notary proclaimed them man and wife.

No thought was given to this arrangement until a few years later when they received a notice from the marriage application department of the State of Tennessee asking them when they planned to get married. They were informed the application would expire in just two weeks. This came as a great surprise to them for they had trusted the counsel of their friend. Now what would they do?

They had been married, they thought, for the past few years so it seemed proper for them to make it right now and finish what they had started. After all, they had enjoyed the last four years and eleven months and fourteen days so why not just continue. The wedding date was set for the following weekend. The local Justice of the Peace was scheduled to perform the ceremony. They were able, also, to roundup a Best Man and a Maid of Honor to accompany the nuptial party. The affair was held at their favorite club. Dinner was served after the wedding and the newlyweds and the wedding party danced the night away after the ceremony. Now that they were really legally married, they would notify the State on the following Monday morning.

Wiley's position as the outside kitchen appliance salesman required him to be on the road five days every week and sometimes six, calling on business owners who handled the company products.

His sales territory covered all of the southeastern states west of the Mississippi river from Tennessee south. He and Maggie were only able to be with each other on the weekends and there were times he could not return to Cleveland at all until the following weekend. On these occasions, he would phone in his orders and his report for the week's activities.

Being a traveling salesperson was the ideal occupation for Wiley because he enjoyed meeting new people and he was pleased with the good salary and expense account that the job provided. In this type of work he made many friends and one of his new friends was to become a real problem for him. One customer in particular owned her own Appliance Specialty Store in Tampa. The owner Thelma Goode was a beautiful outgoing widow about Wiley's age. She seemed to take a liking to Wiley and he had the same opinion of her.

The once a month stopover for this part of his sales route was in Tampa. After he had worked his sales route for a few months, Thelma asked him to have dinner with her after she closed the store for the day. They went to Ybor City and had dinner at the Columbia Restaurant. The dinner was a wonderful treat for Wiley since he had never before experienced the wonderful culinary delights of the Cuban cooking they enjoyed that night.

After dinner they retired to one of the local bistros for a few after-dinner drinks. They were in luck for there was a small dance floor there and a Cuban combo to provide dance music. Wiley could not resist the rhythm of the music and he asked Thelma if she would like to dance. She accepted his offer and they danced away the remainder of the evening. Wiley took her home and she invited him in for a nightcap. Before he left to return to his motel room he asked if he could see her again the following month on his Wednesday visit and her answer was yes.

Now at no time did Wiley indicate in any way to Thelma that he was a married man. After all, Tampa was a long way from Cleveland and Maggie would never miss "a slice off a cut loaf". Being that far separated neither would Thelma know about Maggie and he could play his game of infidelity with no threat of being found out. Little did

Wiley expect that fate was about to throw him a curve ball. Maggie would accidentally discover the truth about his tawdry affair.

On one of Wiley's later visits to the Appliance Specialty Store, Thelma gave him a nice order for toasters, mixers, hot plates and other items that the store needed for Christmas sales. When the order was called in Maggie was working as a fill-in for the shipping clerk. Since the hot plates would not be ready for shipment to meet the requirements of the order, she called Thelma to let her know. Maggie asked if a substitute item would be acceptable and if so which item would she like as a substitute or would she like to wait on a later shipment of the hot plates. Of course, Maggie identified herself with her full name Maggie Comer.

Thelma put two and two together and it dawned on her that the caller was a Comer and Wiley's name was Comer. She wondered if these two could be related. Could they be related as maybe man and wife or brother and sister or perhaps cousins? She would have to ask Wiley about it on his next visit to the store. The question bothered her until Wiley called on her on his next monthly Wednesday visit. How was she to find out the truth without offending him? Of course, if they were not married, it would not matter and she could ask a direct question with no harm done. Should she come right out and ask? And if they were married would he lie about it? Maybe if she just beat around the bush and dropped a hint about the inability of the plant to deliver all the items on the last order, she would learn the truth of the matter. If this approach didn't work she could come right out and tell him she had discussed the matter with their shipping clerk Maggie Comer. Such an approach might bring out the truth by just mentioning that he and the shipping clerk had the same name.

When Thelma finally did ask about his relationship with the shipping clerk, Wiley was stunned. His first thought was how could she have possibly connected with Maggie so easily? Maggie had probably only worked as a relief for the regular clerk for one day and as fate had decreed that was the one day she had to call Thelma about the order.

Now Wiley was really on the horns of a dilemma. Should he just come right out and tell the truth about him and Maggie? If he did, Thelma might drop him like a hot potato and he did not want to lose the comfortable relationship he had been enjoying. He had to think fast as Thelma was sitting there patiently waiting for an answer. On the spur of the moment he said yes she had been his wife until the divorce but now the relationship was over and forgotten. Thelma was somehow not surprised with Wiley's answer but after she had talked with Maggie about the order, she had a gut feeling the two of them were man and wife. She was pretty sure now that Wiley's answer was a lie and there had never been a divorce. He lied thinking Thelma would buy his story and he could continue their affair as it had been on each of his monthly visits.

She had come to enjoy Wiley's monthly store calls and the dinners, the evenings of dancing and the nightcaps at her place afterwards. Thelma knew she would hate to lose Wiley for he was a pleasant companion for the evening, an excellent dancer and he knew how to make a woman love him. It had been several years since she lost her wonderful husband in an accident in the shipyard. He had been a ship fitter and while working on one of the ships under construction, a cable broke on the lifting crane and a steel plate dropped on him, killing him instantly. The accident had occurred five years ago and she had not met anyone she cared to be with until Wiley came on the scene. Now the ball was in Thelma's court. She had to make a decision right now about this matter, this very evening. Knowing what Wiley had told her of his connection with Maggie and what she strongly felt, it might be prudent and wise to make changes in her plans for the evening. She broke the news gently that a situation had occurred on the spur of the moment and therefore it would be impossible for her to be with him this evening. She told him there was no way she could have gotten word to him earlier about the emergency call.

Yes, Wiley was disappointed to say the least for he had been looking forward to this outing in Tampa ever since he was there last month. He managed to mumble something to the effect he was sorry they couldn't have dinner and then took his leave. Thelma's Kitchen Appliance Supply store was his last call in Tampa. He debated with himself if he should return to his motel room and spend a miserable night by himself or would it be best to continue on to Winter Haven, his next point of call. Near midnight Wiley pulled in to the Super Six motel in Winter Haven and spent the remainder of the night.

For the next two days Wiley could think of nothing but how he had failed in Tampa. He wondered how much Thelma really knew about him and Maggie. Did she learn something from the phone call that she didn't tell him? It seemed to him that she knew more than she was willing to say at the time. Wiley's next problem would come when he returned home. If Maggie knew of his affair in Tampa, she would be sure to inform him of the fact and tell him what he could do. Maggie was not one to let things go. She would confront Wiley with it right away.

When Wiley arrived home the following Friday evening Maggie was glad to see him as usual. She wanted to know how his week went and if he was successful in writing many orders for the company products. He was brought up to date about things in the plant and she told him about sitting in for the shipping clerk who was out sick. There was not one word about the call to Thelma. He thought maybe she considered that just one of the mundane tasks the shipping clerk performed every day. Maybe Wiley was safe on the home front for Maggie didn't seem to be concerned about what he might have done while he was away. Wiley and Maggie had always had their own bank accounts, their own autos and they put a certain amount of their earnings in a common account to pay the household expenses. Maggie's pastime was gambling at the slot machines on the casino riverboats and Wiley spent his spare time fishing.

After the scare about being found out in Tampa, Wiley turned over a new leaf. Now he would play it straight. He only had two more years until retirement. He intended to finish his twenty years so he and Maggie could retire together. Wiley knew without a doubt that Maggie was the best thing that ever happened to him and he sure didn't want to lose her. They did both retire and bought a small seaside cottage at Ocean Springs. Here they could indulge in their hobbies at their leisure. For Maggie the Biloxi casinos were just across the new bridge and the opportunities for fishing were endless. Wiley could participate in deep sea fishing from the charter boats in Back Bay or he could fish locally at the beach or in the bay. It was the best of both worlds for them and they lived a long and satisfying time in retirement.

Mary was the next Smith girl. Her turn to leave home came when she graduated from high school during World War II and joined the Women's Army Corps. Her basic training Army camp was located in Augusta, Georgia. She spent six months there. She did really well on the Army intelligence tests. Her score was above 125 points, high enough for her to qualify to attend officer candidate school. After she finished basic training, she made application for officer training and was accepted and transferred to the school at Carlisle Barrack. The school was four months of very rigorous training including classroom studies during the day covering all the subjects an Army officer should know.

Army administration is one subject that all successful officer candidates must be well trained in before they can graduate and be commissioned. The management and discipline of Army personnel was stressed in all of her classes, which is a basic function of officers in the military. Another course that was most important was the operation and maintenance of the mess hall where food was prepared, dispensed and where high standards of sanitation must be maintained to safeguard the health of the troops. There were orientations on how to protect the troops in a combat area and how field camps were to be prepared.

Each morning there was an hour of calisthenics in order to exercise properly and to stay fit for service. Marching formations and close-order drills were practiced one day each week. Only the best would be able to graduate from the course and be commissioned. An average class of school candidates would have approximately 50% of the students drop out for one cause or another. Many of the dropouts were because of discipline problems. Some students could not or would not adhere to the very strict rules of the school. Approximately 10% of the students could not comprehend the training courses, and these, also, would fail to graduate.

Mary graduated at the top of her class and received a commission as a Second Lieutenant in the Women's Army Corps. It was suggested at the school that those graduating with high scores could apply for an additional school if they wished to become specialists instead of going in for troop duty. Mary applied to attend the Judge Advocate General School at Petersburg, where she would spend three months studying personnel management and personnel classification. The course prepared her to become a personnel officer. She would see to the personnel records, maintain the daily reports and oversee the classification of personnel.

Upon graduation from the school, she was assigned to duty as the personnel officer of the General Hospital at Fort Devens. A Women's Army Corps company of troops was stationed at the hospital and they worked at various duties to support the medical personnel, including operating the hospital library. All of the patients records were managed by the women and many of the women were trained as hospital technicians. They managed the mess hall and the feeding of the patients in the hospital wards. It was a good duty station. Everyone liked the duty and the location of the Fort, which was just a short train ride into Boston. There was a nice officers' club and a very nice enlisted men's and women's club. These clubs provided excellent entertainment for the troops during off-duty hours.

After serving two years as a personnel officer at Lovell General Hospital, Mary was promoted to First Lieutenant. A vacancy came open at General Hospital at Waltham, for a personnel officer. She applied for the transfer and it was granted. It was a much larger hospital and the personnel officer's position called for a Captain's rating. If Mary could fill the position and did an excellent job, she could be promoted at the end of her first year in the new job. This was an excellent opportunity for her and she was promoted to Captain.

67

Now she was getting up in the world, and in the Army. She might decide to remain in the service until retirement.

Mary had spent the post-World War II years at The General Hospital and had gained much knowledge in her field of endeavor and now she was ready for a new assignment. She soon received an opportunity to go overseas as the Korean War or as the politicians called it "police action" had just begun in June, 1950. When soldiers were wounded, they were moved from Korea to Japan for hospitalization and for rest and recuperation. There was a need for Mary's personnel skills over there. She applied for overseas duty, and was shipped out and assigned to the Army hospital in Tokyo, Japan.

Her assignment in Japan was as Company Commander of a Women's Army Corps Company that handled all the administrative duties of the Rest and Recuperation unit of the hospital. The unit also handled the processing and shipment of the wounded back to the States. After four years of service in Japan, she had been reassigned from the Company Commander position to a staff assignment with the Headquarters Division of the hospital. As a member of the hospital staff she was promoted to Major.

She returned to the States when her tour of duty was completed in Japan and was assigned to the Staff of the Women's Army Corps Headquarters in Washington, D.C. Her duties there were to develop training methods for future personnel officers. This was good duty, and living in Washington was most interesting. On weekends, she could go into nearby New York City, see the Broadway plays, and visit the many tourist sights. She remained at Washington until the outbreak of the Vietnam War (or as the politicians chose to refer to this one also, a police action, not a war.

Again, Mary chose to go overseas. This time is was to Saigon to work in the Army Hospital. She was in charge of the disposition of wounded military personnel, caring for their records and arranging transportation for those that needed to be returned to the States for further treatment. In all of her military career this was one of the toughest due to the location in the tropics and the number of serious war injuries.

After three years in Vietnam she was ready to retire. She had her twenty years in and was now eligible to be promoted to Lieutenant Colonel in the Reserve Army as soon as she made application for retirement and returned to the States. She was just over forty years of age. Now she could take life easy and that is what she planned to do, settling in a beach condo on the Gulf of Mexico at Gulfport, Mississippi.

After a few weeks, the inactivity began to get to Mary. She became restless and needed something meaningful to do each day. She had always wished to go to college when she finished high school but it was not possible at the time. Now that she was entitled to the benefits of the G.I. Bill that provided a college education and many other benefits for retired military personnel, it might be a good thing to take advantage of these opportunities. She would look into entering college and studying for a degree in liberal arts.

She applied at the University of Southern Mississippi and was accepted to begin classes in the fall semester. It was fun going back to school even though she was older than most of the students. Maybe she would be a better student than the younger ones, because she knew why she was there and she studied hard in order to make good grades. There was no need to go to school if you didn't intend to study and learn. Diligence helped her attain good grades. Her first year at the university, she was on the Dean's List. She found that going to school was easy if you were attentive in class and studied.

By the time she reached her senior year and was ready to graduate, she had become a real pro and had an excellent scholastic achievement record. She graduated summa cum laude and was one of the officers of her senior class.

It was time now, after graduation, to determine what she wanted do next. Would she go back to loafing on the beach and enjoying the idleness of her coastal life or would she put her new-found knowledge to work? It would be nice, she thought, if she could get a job in Federal Civil Service. Then after ten years on the job she could retire again and increase her income. The common reference to such deals was to become a "double-dipper". This was a situation where one could retire twice from government service and draw a pension from each retirement. This is what she decided to do. She placed her application with the Civil Service and was soon on the list to be hired.

It had been quite a while since Mary had seen her sisters and brothers since she had been overseas for so many years. While she was waiting for an opening to come up in government Civil Service, it would be a good time for her to do some visiting and find out how her siblings were getting along. She could also spend some time with her mother who was getting up in years and who was in poor health. She would have to do some traveling for her siblings were spread out over Alabama, Mississippi, Tennessee and Georgia. It would take some time but she would try to stay with each of them for a few days so she could find out how they all were getting along.

There were also cousins in Texas and Virginia that she had not seen since they were children together. Her mother's two oldest brothers had moved to Texas during the Depression in order to find jobs. The oldest had managed to get a job in Virginia in the mid-1930s and had remained employed there until he retired after the Korean War. He married a beautiful young Polish girl and they raised their family of three girls and three boys in a small town just outside of Richmond. Mary had not seen any of these family members since she was a teenager so it would be nice to drop by and visit with them.

Her mother's next oldest brother migrated to Columbus during the Depression and found a job as a policeman for the city of Columbus. He remained on this job for thirty years and when he retired he was the Chief of Police. Mary had not seen his family of three boys and one girl since the little blonde haired girl was four years of age. The little girl had come with one of her cousins to visit her grandmother so many years ago. One of the boys of the family had moved to Minnesota when he graduated from high school and no one had seen him in some time. They were never sure what happened to him. The other son married a girl from Texas and they moved to there to live with her folks on a big Texas ranch.

Mary spent six weeks visiting with her sisters and brothers traveling from one to the other and now it was time to return to the

Mississippi Gulf Coast and the condo and rest up before starting another project or going on a new job. An opening came within the next month after her return from visiting the kinfolks. The opening was for a position at the Mississippi Space Center located just north of Pascagoula. She got back into her old specialty in her new position, for she was in the personnel department and interviewing prospective employees. The new job was ideal and she continued in it until she retired the second time.

Leatha was the baby of the Smith family and the most beautiful, with black curly hair, baby blue eyes. She always had an infectious smile. Her mother and father were both Irish and she inherited all the beautiful Irish features. At eighteen, when she graduated from high school, she was five foot four inches tall and weighed one hundred ten. She was one of the honor students in school, sang in the choir at the local Methodist church and sang solos at weddings and funerals. While she was a teenager, she helped in the fields and one of her jobs was picking worms off tobacco plants, not the most pleasant job, but it had to be done.

After she graduated from high school the war was just getting started in Europe and the government was thinking of war and making preparations just in case the war came to the States. Grants were being made available to high school graduates to attend a six-month technical school to learn a trade that would be needed in wartime production. Leatha applied and was sent to a technical school where she learned to be an aircraft mechanic. By the time she finished school the draft for military service had begun and factories and shipyards were geared up for production. The plants were producing aircraft and ships for the Allies.

These young technical graduates were assigned jobs in the various industries that were producing war material. Leatha received orders to report to Fort Whiting located. She was processed to be a mechanic on the assembly line where aircraft engines were being overhauled. The new employees attended classes the first four hours of the day and the last four hours of the day they worked under supervision in the repair hangar. The work was easy and the pay was good for the times, and relative to the skill of the employee.

Dormitories were set up in town near the Field for the workers and Leatha lived in one of them with nine other young ladies. They were furnished a bed and a space and two meals per day. Lunch had to be provided by the girls at their work site. The congregate living was not to Leatha's liking and she soon found a more suitable place to live. An old couple had a café at the street corner near the dormitory and she was able to rent their extra room. This worked out well for her as the old couple was delighted to have a young lady in the house and they provided meals for her. The location of the café was on the corner where the bus stop was and it was very handy to get to work. Now Leatha had someone to look after her, and it was a good situation.

In time, the old couple came to take care of her as if she was their own daughter. Leatha had, in the past, a few bouts with an inflamed appendix and soon she had a serious attack. Her landlady called the nurse at the Field. She came and admitted her to the hospital where the appendix was removed. Leatha's mother came down and stayed with her for the remainder of the week until she was back on her feet. The old man and old lady were good to her and she lived there with them until the war was over. At work she had a good supervisor. He was an older man who was from her home town and he looked after her while she was on the job. When the Base was about to close at the end of the war he saw that she was one of the last employees to be laid off. When she was laid off and the Base closed, she went home and spent some time with her mother. Sam had long since passed away, so she didn't have any worry about dealing with him anymore. She had saved her money while she was working but she now she wanted to get another job. A visit to her aunt and uncle in Birmingham gave her a chance to look for work up there. The first day she put in an application, she was hired as a clerk. After a few weeks on the job she decided this was not for her and she returned to Mobile.

This time she rented a room with an old, widowed woman who lived on Old Shell Road near Broad. She was French and she was a seamstress. This lady had been a resident of Mobile all her life and she knew everyone of any consequence. She suggested to Leatha that she apply at the local bank for she had heard they needed a secretary in the loan department. Leatha dressed in her prettiest dress and went to the bank. They hired her right then and there. It was a good job and she got to meet some very nice people. Pretty soon everyone, especially the young single men in the bank, knew about that pretty little blue-eyed girl in the loan department.

It wasn't very long before she got to know everyone that worked in the bank and one young man in particular, Wilbur Tomson. He worked upstairs in the Bond Department. His family was quite wealthy. They owned shares in the bank and young Wilbur owned his own airplane and a boat which he kept at the river landing. This young man thought there was no one as beautiful as Leatha. Every weekend she was invited to a movie or to a dance or just for a ride to Hattiesburg in his plane. At other times they go out on his boat. She had to think twice about continuing to date Wilbur for he was the jealous type and did not want anyone to look at his girlfriend, let alone have a dance with her at a party. He had asked her to marry him but she could not. She felt that he was too far out of her class for them to ever be a happy married couple. She felt she could never fit in his world and she could not abide his being so jealous without a cause. He was six years older than Leatha but he was not mature and settled. It wasn't very long until she had to tell him she couldn't see him anymore.

Pretty soon another man entered her life. His name was Thomas Wadkins. He was to become a real problem for Leatha. He was a veteran of World War II who had served in the Pacific. He worked as mechanic in the shipyard. The first six months, they spent much time together getting to know each other. Later she realized that she didn't really get to know him at all. She just thought she did. On some of the subjects she asked about he was quite vague. Suddenly one day, he had asked her to marry him and on the spur of the moment she accepted. They drove over to Hattiesburg that weekend, got married and moved into the small apartment where she had a room. Things were going pretty well until his father came over and moved in with them. There really wasn't room in the small apartment for the three of them but they managed. Then when his mother came over to visit with her husband and her son, it really was a mess. Finally after two weeks his mother and father went back to Mississippi where they had a home.

Leatha had made plans for the two of them to buy a piece of property out west of the city and get a government loan through the G.I. Bill for veterans and build a home. They picked out a lot and she gave Thomas money to go and buy it. He was gone all day and when he came back that evening she asked if he had bought the lot and he told her he did not. She asked what he did with the money. He told her he went and paid up some of his bills. Now this was a hell of a note, first that the information about his previous marriage should come out at this late date. And second, what else did she need to know? He told her the whole tawdry tale how his first wife had acted and how she treated him.

Two weeks later he got a job as a mechanic at a shop on the coast in Mississippi. He suggested that Leatha quit her bank job and move to Mississippi and they would live in the big house owned by his father. She reluctantly moved into the house with his father and older sister but there was room for the whole gang. Leatha was now pregnant. The baby was coming soon and the extended family could help with raising the little one.

Thomas worked at the shop on the coast, driving there and back each day. Things worked out pretty well for the first six months and then he began to be very late getting home at night claiming he had to work extra to get the jobs out. Then he began to have jobs out of town that would keep him away from home all night. She was commencing to believe that there was a "skunk in the woodpile" somewhere. She eventually discovered there was a young woman who kept the books at the shop and she turned out to be the cause of his keeping late hours and his failure to get home some nights.

Wadkins had told the bookkeeper at the shop that his wife had a pen full of chickens. She asked if she could get some chicken shit to fertilize her garden. He told her she would have to ask his wife. A few days later she showed up at Leatha's house with two big buckets asking for the chicken shit. Leatha knew who she was and this was just too much. For the time being she was sharing her husband but she sure wasn't about to share her chicken shit. When asked if she could have two buckets full Leatha told her "the chickens have quit shitting and I don't have any to spare". The bookkeeper got in her car and took off.

While Thomas worked as a mechanic, he had made contact with the southern branch of an automobile recovery business and now they contacted him to set up a shop. They would finance everything and he was to be their southern source of vehicle recovery. He would do the modifications, repairs, painting and delivery of the vehicles before they were returned to their rightful owners.

Thomas located a large shop with an upstairs apartment. He fitted out the shop with the necessary equipment and bought a large towing vehicle. The Company provided all the funds necessary for setting up the shop. He started getting calls such to go out to San Francisco and pick up a red Cadillac, take it to the shop, repaint it and when it was done to deliver it to its rightful owner in Miami. Now Thomas was seldom home.

Leatha had to find a job. She could not just sit and wait for him to come and then leave out again two days later. She bought a car and found a job at the local manufacturing plant. To help pay for the car and the gasoline, she took four riders with her to work each day. One morning she came out to get into her car to go to work and it was gone. Thomas was asked where her car was, and he told her he had sold it during the night because he needed money. He was behind again in his payments. She used his car to go to work and she made him buy her another car the next day. The situation was getting serious. She had no idea how long she would be able to put up with this sort of thing. Here was a man who was irresponsible and one that could not be depended on for anything.

These charades on the part of Thomas had been going on now for five years and things were not getting better. They were getting worse. The straw that broke the camel's back came early one morning

75

when Leatha got a phone call from a young girl asking her if she knew where her husband was. The caller told Leatha she knew. He was in bed with her mother and had been there all night. Leatha gathered up all of his clothes, put them in the car and took them to the house where Thomas was shacked-up. She drove into the driveway, blew the horn, threw all his clothes on the ground and drove off. That day she filed for divorce and moved out.

She and her five year old son moved into a small home in the north side of town. Her job at the manufacturing plant would pay the bills until she could get a divorce settlement. The two of them did all right and on Sunday they attended church together. For five years they lived on their own. Leatha had met a nice man at church, who was a member of her Sunday school class. He was a widower and had two small children. His wife had been killed in an automobile accident just the year before. Maybe it was sympathy for him on Leatha's part and a need for a mother for his children on his part that the two of them gravitated towards each other. Some of Leatha's friends seemed to think he was a good Christian man. He owned a business and lived in a nice house in the nice section of town.

Very soon Leatha and Oscar Wilkes were married. His young children took to Leatha just as if she was their natural mother, and she loved them. It wasn't long before she discovered the truth. He was part owner of a bar on the north side of town and he had waitresses who sometimes did double duty. During the days, he delivered groceries to various vendors throughout the county. He was up early and came in late after he had stopped by the bar. Sometimes it was in the wee hours of the morning when he came in and he would be soaked to the ears in booze. Most of the time he drank in the evenings while at the bar and when he arrived at home he was drunk and quarrelsome.

Every Sunday after they were married, Leatha had to stay at home and prepare Sunday dinner for Oscar, his sister and her family and his mother. They all went to church but Leatha had to stay and prepare a big meal for his relatives. Sometimes there would be fifteen or more to feed on Sunday. After the meal, she had to clean up the kitchen and the dishes for none of the relatives would help to do anything. This got to be a real problem and she told Oscar that she would cook for the family but not all of his family. They could either help so she could go to church or they would have to eat at home. He finally told his family they could not come there every Sunday for a free meal.

Leatha took good care of his children and got them off to school every morning but she couldn't tolerate the way Oscar treated her son. The night Oscar came in drunk and slung his wet coat across her face and started to rant and rave was the last straw. The next morning after he left for work Leatha and her son picked up their things and moved out for the time being. She filed for divorce that same day. As soon as the divorce was final, she managed to buy a home on the west side of town.

Within a few days she had a job at the local hospital where she was training to be a Licensed Practical Nurse. After the completion of a six-month training period she qualified to get her license as LPN. It was only a few days before one of her supervisors let her know that there was a position open with the local hospital's nursing department, for a person with her qualifications. If Leatha wanted the job she would be glad to recommend her. The job was open and it would be best if she went that very afternoon to apply. She went for the interview and was hired that day, and started to work the following day.

Now she would have a good salary and could provide for herself and her son, Wayne, and manage to pay the bills if she were frugal. She worked hard at her new job and they were satisfied with her work. To help pay the bills, she took in sewing for she was an expert seamstress and she made gowns for the ladies in the Mardi Gras parades. When her son reached sixteen, he just had to have an automobile. It was not a luxury that she could afford but she took on more evening and weekend work sitting with old folks who couldn't be left alone, and got the money for the car.

Wayne was getting to be a big boy now. His mother indulged him and catered to his every whim for he was the only thing that

Leatha could really call her own. She also thought Wayne was someone who would never leave her. His steady diet was fattening foods and soft drinks. Since there was nothing for him to do around the house on weekends when he was not in school, he just sat around and watched television while his mother worked.

After graduation from high school, Wayne found a job working with a construction company but they were on a job out of town, and he wanted to be home with his mother and eat her home-cooked meals. It wasn't long before he quit and came home. Several other jobs that he was able to get were the same. He just had to be at home so his mother could take care of him and feed him what he wanted to eat. Seems the only thing that he was good at was to gather miscellaneous items and sell them on the weekends at the flea market. This brought in some money but he managed to spend it faster than he could make it.

On week days, he was at home sitting in front of the television and entertaining his friends who hung out in the neighborhood. These friends were mostly girls. They would come and spend the day with him while his mother was at work. When Leatha sat with the elderly all night, the girls would spend the night with Wayne. Many times they were still asleep there when she came in from work and she had to shoo them out and send them back home.

Leatha had now been divorced from her second husband for eight years and she was doing well at her job as a nurse. Most of her work was in the field taking care of home-bound patients. She went from one patient to another caring for the bedridden, bathing them, checking their vital signs, giving them their medicine and making reports on the patient's progress. Along with her salary and her extra work she felt she could buy a larger home. She found one she could handle the payments for and planned to sell the smaller home.

There was just not enough space in the small house for her to be comfortable when Wayne had his friends in until the wee hours of the morning. She had to be able to get her good night's sleep for the following work day. After she got the larger home Wayne would not move. He said he had to stay there where he could be with his friends in the neighborhood. Now she had two house payments to make each month and she was already on a tight budget. She could not bear to deny her baby boy anything, so she would just have to find a way to meet the new demands.

Soon after moving to the new home, Leatha found that she had another problem. Wayne was now going to be the father of a baby by one of the girls in the neighborhood. Child support had to be paid once the baby was born. Wayne was not working, had no income to amount to anything and he didn't plan to find a job. If child support was not paid then Wayne would go to jail until he could pay the support. Never could Leatha allow her baby boy to go through this sort of thing. She would just have to find a way to pay the child support for him.

She did find extra work to fill her Saturdays and Sundays. She was able to work as a product demonstrator in grocery stores. That brought enough extra money in for the child support if she could work regularly.

Wayne had already developed diabetes and a heart condition since he was now so overweight. She applied for SSI disability payments for him, which would also provide him with free medical care and an income to pay part of his bills. The payments were approved within the next six months and now he had an income of $500 a month and his medical bills would be paid.

This was a great relief because Leatha also needed medical care, but she couldn't stop work long enough to go to the hospital for surgery and treatment. She had no one to care for Wayne, who was quickly becoming bedridden. The doctors had told her that she must have heart surgery as there was a family history of heart problems and she had clogged arteries that must be cleared with stents. Such surgery would take at least a week of hospital care and home recuperation before she could return to work and she kept putting it off.

Wayne's condition continued to worsen and he was in the hospital once or twice each month. He now had asthma and Chronic Obstructive Pulmonary Disease and had to be on oxygen twenty-four hours a day. After two years of his being in and out of the hospital, she had to move him against his will to her house, so she could look after him at night without her having to go out.

The county medical service saw to his daily nurse visits while his mother was at work. Five days a week the visiting nurse would come in and bath him, check his vital signs and give him his medicine and shots. He was steadily getting worse and there seemed to be no help coming from the hospital and doctors' visits. At the hospital, they just kept him for a few days then sent him home. At least every two weeks he had to go to the hospital to be cleared up so he could breathe and again they would keep him a few days and send him home again.

The hospital trips continued for about a year and then one afternoon, he commenced to have breathing problems and an ambulance was called. They arrived within minutes, but he was already passed out. Emergency resuscitation did no good and in moments he was gone. His death was a great shock to Leatha for she had always said he would overcome these problems and one day be back on his feet. Wayne was all she ever had that she could call her own. She had two tough marriages, neither of which was anything but trouble. Could the Lord be trying to tell her something?

Why was she being punished like this? First it was the philandering husband who couldn't be trusted, and then the drunken sadist, and now her only real possession had been taken from her. Leatha had retired the year before her son was taken but she was still having problems paying bills so she was continuing to work on the weekends. She was still sitting with the elderly and looking after them at times when needed.

There were nagging problems with her health, since she still had not taken care of the heart surgery that was needed. To add to her problems she still had two mortgages to pay on each month and she received a letter from the mortgage holder saying that insurance rates were being increased. At present the insurance on the homes was a modest $400 per year. The new insurance rates would be $200 per month. The news of the rate increases was devastating as there was no way she could pay it on her modest retirement.

Help was to come from an undreamed of source, her neighbor who lived across the street. He was a widower, and an old friend from 1942 when she worked at Brookley Field. She told her story to him and he suggested a solution. He could lend her enough to pay off the small house since she no longer had a need for it. Then she could sell it. The sale of the house would provide enough for her to pay off the house she was living in and repay his loan. She agreed to his generous offer and so could finally take it easy. With no house or car payments, she would not have to work unless she wished to do so.

She continued to do the demonstration work because she enjoyed being out and meeting the public but one day she passed out on the job. It just happened that the widower from across the street, Richard Evans, walked in as the store manager was about to call an ambulance. Richard put her in his car and took her to the emergency room. She was treated and the doctor insisted she have a heart catheter while she was there. In the process, she had a heart attack while in the doctor's office. She was sent immediately up to the operating room for heart surgery. Richard stayed with her and cared for her while she was recuperating. He also took care of her cat and dog while she was away. A week in the hospital and she was ready to come home. It was fortunate that she got to the hospital when she did and had the heart surgery otherwise she would not have lasted very long.

After a few weeks recuperation, she was feeling much better but now instead of going back to work she planned to enjoy the years that she had remaining. She had her home paid for and enough money coming in from her retirement so that she didn't have to work. Every day she and Richard went someplace, a trip to the Mall for lunch, a ride out to the beach just to stroll on the white sand or a trip to the ice cream parlor for a cone of pistachio ice cream. Occasionally the two of them made a trip to the casinos in Biloxi. It made for a nice outing and sometimes they would win. On the first trip to the casino, she kept asking herself, "what is this guy up to" and "what is he planning?" Later when she got to know him better, she told him that she was expecting him to stop at a motel for a while on the way back home, but he never did. She and Richard were getting rather close now, but she had said to herself years earlier that she would never attempt another marriage.

Now for the past six months she was thinking that maybe with Richard things would be different. He had been so much help when she was in need. He was not a womanizer, or a drunk and he seemed to be well- mannered. Would a marriage with him work out and not end in disaster as the other two had done? There were indications he wanted to remarry after the loss of his wife of fifty years; in fact, he had asked if she knew of any eligible widows that might be looking for another mate. Was this an invitation for her to volunteer? Maybe so. She would think about it.

In September that year, the hurricane came, the first that had hit the area in years. With the hurricane came tornados and both her house and Richard's house were demolished. They lost nearly everything and there was nothing to do but to salvage what they could and sell what was left of the two homes. Now it became quite clear that they needed each other more than ever. They decided to get married and then find a new home out of the hurricane area and settle in for the remainder of their days. Two weeks after the hurricane blew through town they were married.

They moved what they had to South Alabama and found a new home and moved in. But all was not well. Leatha had been suffering from acute asthma for a number of years. The wetness and mold from the storm had aggravated the asthma condition. She was hospitalized shortly after moving into the new house. On the second trip to the hospital, it was found she had to have two stents put in her heart. The heart surgery did not do the complete job. Now she was on several types of medication. Richard was taking care of her, doing the cooking and housework so she could recuperate. At one point, she felt well enough for them to drive to Biloxi to the casino. While they were there, she won enough to buy a registered miniature poodle. She always wanted one but could never afford it until now. It was a pretty thing, six weeks old.

The following year housing became available in Pensacola and they sold the house in South Alabama and found a nice home in

82

Pensacola. Soon it became necessary that she go to the emergency room every week or so. The medicine the doctor was prescribing did little or no good to relieve her asthma. Even with the regular hospital visits and the doctor visits she was not getting any better. Shortly after she got her pretty poodle puppy, she passed away quietly in her sleep just before her eighty-eighth birthday. She had outlived her entire family. Her trials in life were many but she finally overcame them all and succeeded in the end.

In Memoriam

To Leatha Smith

Many were her earthly problems.
The Devil taunted her every way she turned in life.
Through her Christian love she met and conquered
Every challenge that came her way.
Many were her burdens, more than she should have had.
Her entire life was given to helping others.
Seldom was this favor returned.
She is at home in Heaven now,
Oh so happy and so bright
Where there is joy and beauty
In that everlasting light.

Chapter Five

The Noles Family

    The Noles home was a large residence set high on a hill overlooking the vast acreage of their farm. It had been built at the turn of the century of the finest hardwood finished lumber. The high pitched roof was covered in sheet iron and there were lightning rods to protect the home from lightning strikes during bad weather. It was one of the finest houses in the area and was painted with white lead paint.

In contrast with the poor small farmer who barely made a living for his family, this is the story of a large farmer who tilled many acres, made big money and should have been immune to some of the problems of the times.

No one, it seemed, could escape the wrath of the Depression years, even those who had large holdings and the potential to be able to survive under almost any circumstances. The only difference between the haves and the have-nots was that one had more to lose than the other.

Richard Noles owned a 300 acre farm located in the poorest county in central Alabama, which had been in his family since before the Civil War. His grandfather had purchased the land for fifty cents an acre in 1842. It was good land and a great deal of it was bottom land that lay along Mulberry Creek which ran through the lower 200 acres. Richard had inherited the land from his father in 1890. Most of the land was cleared and 100 acres were fenced and seeded each year to provide pasture for the livestock.

Besides the old Noles home, there were four sharecropper houses on the property for members of the family who worked the farm with their father. The oldest Noles daughter, with her family, lived in the old "dogtrot" house just below the barns in the peach orchard at the corner of the millet field. Patrick, the third son, and his family lived in the log house over by the creek in the far corner of the property by the sugar cane fields. Oscar Kemp, a cousin, and his family lived in the small house over the hill behind the barns. Clayton and his family lived in the old house at the top of the hill at the south end of the property.

Near the back door of the kitchen at the main home there was a large garden and fruit orchard. There were apples, peaches, grapes, plums and apricots that provided plenty of fresh fruit in season and plenty of fruit to dry for the winter months. The vegetable garden covered several acres and provided plenty of vegetables for all the families living on the farm. There were a 2 acre melon patch and a 2 acre strawberry patch in addition to the garden. The main Noles home was a large ten room house with a high gabled roof and porches all around. A main hallway ran all the way through the house from the front to the back porch. On the back porch was a deep well for drawing water. The house was illuminated by carbide gas lamps and a large carbide generator tank was set in the corner of the front yard. There were four large fireplaces that heated the entire home. In the kitchen, there were two large cast iron wood burning cook stoves and a twenty foot long dining table. This large kitchen provided plenty of space to feed the workers when they came in from the field for everyone working in the fields; men, women, and children, always ate at the Noles house.

There were three large two story barns, a large cow lot, another large lot for the horses and mules, and a pig pen located down the dirt road a few hundred yards from the house. The farm equipment was kept in two large sheds that ran the length of the barnyard and the blacksmith shop was located under a large red oak tree across the road from the barns. Lighting for the barns was also provided by the carbide gas system. There was a well and watering troughs located at the corner of the dairy barn for watering the stock.

It was there in the barnyard after breakfast every morning where each of the field hands would receive his special assignment for the day's work. Some would hitch up the mules and plow, others would spread fertilizer as the crops began to grow, and others would thin the cotton and the corn. The assignment of each field worker changed with the seasons. Planting time was a busy job for everyone. Then when the crops matured there was a slack time and the workers could relax some in preparation for the harvest.

The fall of the year, usually late September, was the time for syrup-making. First the sorghum syrup would be made and then the cane syrup. The syrup mill was setup on the banks of the creek and there was a juice mill that was turned by a mule that traveled around in a circle pulling a long wooden beam attached to the cane mill rollers. Cane stalks were fed into the mill as it turned and the juice was collected in a barrel located under the mill.

The juice was cooked down in a copper pan that was 4 feet wide and 8 feet long. It was set up under a metal roof over a long fire pit.

87

Juice was fed into one end of the pan where it flowed alternately from one side of the pan to the other as it boiled. By the time the boiled juice reached the lower end of the pan it had thickened and had become syrup. The syrup was then drawn from the cooking pan and sealed in new one gallon metal cans.

The key to making excellent quality sorghum or cane syrup was the experienced syrup maker. He was normally one of the older farmers of the area who had been making syrup for many years. This person would have worked with an experienced syrup maker for several seasons before being allowed to work by himself.

The most important step in the process of making the sweet elixir from the cane and the sorghum was the juice had to be moved from the cool end of the cooking pan to the hot end of the pan continuously. Should the juice stay too long in one area of the pan it was likely to be burned or under-cooked. Either condition would cause the finished syrup to taste bad, be too thin or too thick. At the lower end of the cooking pan the syrup had to be watched very closely in order to keep it from burning for this was the area where the sugar in the syrup was most highly concentrated. A good syrup maker knew just how to keep the juice moving at all times in order to make the finest syrup.

As the juice commenced to boil, there would be foam produced over the cooking pan. This foam had to be removed so that the finished syrup would be clear and there would be no after-taste. The removal of the foam was a constant job for one of the helpers at the cooking pan and it was normally performed by an apprentice. The foam was skimmed off and placed in a barrel for further use. This foam was later used to provide the sugar to make corn liquor. Each year the family would make two barrels of corn liquor to provide sipping whiskey and for medicinal purposes as needed. These two barrels would be secreted away in the hay loft of one of the barns and only the elder Noles was allowed to tap the barrels.

At harvest time everyone including the young children was in the fields picking peas, picking cotton, harvesting watermelons and pulling corn. On a large farm everyone had work to do. There was seldom a time when any member of the group would be idle with nothing to do. When the fruit in the orchard was ripe, the small children were put to work peeling apples and peaches for drying and canning. One or two of the teenage daughters would be assigned to Amanda Noles in the kitchen in order to learn cooking and to help with preparing the food for the field workers. When the big dinner bell was rung the food would be waiting in the kitchen for the workers from the fields.

The Richard Noles family consisted of his wife Amanda, who was known to everyone as Mandy, and ten children of which five were boys and five girls. Richard's father was a Civil War veteran and Richard was born after the war in 1868. His wife Mandy was from a Birmingham family who were early settlers in Alabama. Her family had come into the area before Alabama became a state. Her maiden name was Jones. Her ancestors moved to the Alabama territory in 1795, when white settlers had to have a pass from the Chief of the Creek Nations to live in Indian Territory. Her family also fought in the Confederate Army during the Civil War.

Since both families lost relatives in the Civil War, they were very much against war in general. When war broke out in Europe in the First World War, they did everything they could to prevent their two oldest sons from being drafted into service. The oldest son, Robert William, was shipped off to Hot Springs, Arkansas, to take the hot baths since his doctor was convinced it would cure his asthma. No one was sure that Robert William ever had asthma or any kind of disease or ailment. But the ruse worked and he never had to enter the military.

Clayton, the second son, had been bitten by a timber rattler while working in the field when he was a teenager. He almost died, but after two years of recuperation, he was able to walk, though he was definitely not physically able to be in the military service, so he was exempt. The next son was too young to be in the service so none of the boys were in the First World War.

During the World War I years, there was a good market for all farm products and the prices were good. The Noles family did well.

They were able to make money on every crop that was planted. These were the years that enabled Noles to put away money in the bank for the hard times. The market for farm products was still good after World War I because there was a need for food to send to the European countries devastated by war.

Even during the early years of the 1920s, the prices for cotton, corn and other farm products was still good and farmers could make a profit by farming. By the mid-1920s, farm product prices began to drop and they continued to drop until the stock market failed in October of 1929. After that there was no market to speak of in farm products. It became not worth the effort and expense to farm.

Many farmers struggled with mortgage payments, taxes and the high cost of fertilizer and in the late 1920s, there were numerous foreclosures of mortgaged farms. The Noles were fortunate to have enough money in the bank to ride out the bad years of the time even after the fall of the market, but there were worse years to come in the near future. They struggled with low farm income during the first two years of the 1930s. When the banks failed in 1932, it was the end of road for the Noles family. Their bank account was wiped out and there was no money to make payment of taxes or to pay on the mortgage.

The bankers holding the mortgage showed no mercy and the Noles farm was foreclosed. They lost all the land and property except for 200 acres that were not mortgaged. It was the property across Mulberry Creek where the old log house was located. It was fortunate that it was not included in the mortgage for now the family had somewhere to go and to make an effort to start over. They were able to sell some of the tools and livestock but prices were low and they received only a pittance for them. There were peach trees on the log cabin property and most of the 200 acres was cleared. It was mostly bottom land. The family at least had enough resources to become subsistence farmers and to provide for their own existence.

Starting over for the Noles family was hard to take but then there was no other way to turn. The whole country was locked into a deep Depression. There were many people who had no place to live

90

and no way to turn. They, at least, had a home and property, owned free and clear. Crops were planted in the spring to feed the family; the peach crop could possibly bring in a few dollars for buying the essentials that could not be grown on the farm. The youngest sons would live with the family but the other share-croppers would have to find places of their own. Relocation of these families would be difficult, at best, as we will see later on in the story.

After the bank closings and the election in 1932 the "do-nothing President", Herbert Hoover was voted out of office. Hoover did not believe that the government should provide for the people with government funds. His theory was that private enterprise should provide for the people and government should stay out of the rescue mission to help people during the Depression.

The newly elected President, Franklin Roosevelt, saw things quite differently. He knew that the government must step in and do what was needed to improve the situation. In 1933, he began many government work programs to relieve some of the unemployment. Government food programs were started so men could work and get money for groceries. Young men could join the Civilian Conservation Corps where they would be paid for building new parks and recreation areas. Artists were provided jobs to decorate public building and produce other types of art works. Photographers were hired to document the story of the Depression years with photographs. Authors were given work to write and document the stories of the dreadful times. Slowly these government efforts were paying off for some of the unemployed were now able to work and feed their families.

The eldest daughter of the Noles family was Lucinda, known as Lucy. She was still a teenager and the first to be married. Her husband, Rufus Gandy, was an itinerant musician who played the guitar, fiddle and five-string banjo at the various Saturday night dances and hoe-downs around the community. He was not an individual who had any plans for working in the fields or doing any sort of hard labor.

After their marriage, they moved in with his mother and father and he continued to pursue his musical endeavors. That sort of work did not bring enough money to be of much use in providing for a family and the children that followed the marriage. Before long, Lucy was forced to support the family by working for the neighbors in the fields or whatever sort of work she could find.

The couple continued to live with Rufus's family until the children were big enough to work in the fields with their mother. Lucy managed to get a place of their own, by the time the children reached their teen years. With the help of the children, she was able to support the family along with what little help she could get from her husband.

When the oldest of her children, Charles, reached eighteen he joined the Civilian Conservation Corps. It didn't pay very much but the money that he received as a salary was sent home every month to his mother. He didn't really have any need for food; clothing or entertainment for it was all furnished at the camp. Most of the CCC work camps were out in the forest and away from any place to spend money.

The next to leave home was the second oldest Noles daughter, Susan. She married Tom Kendrick when she was 16 years old. Tom was a young man of promise and the two of them moved out and became a share-cropper with Tom's grandfather. It was a good marriage and the two of them did well even in these times of the Depression years. Before long they were able to rent their own land and become successful subsistence farmers. After two years, they were able to have her mother and father move in with them which provided them with more help on the farm. Her father was still playing music when he could find a gig but he still could not bring in any money to speak of to help with the well-being of the family. Susan's younger brother Harold Noles was now old enough to be of help on the farm. Her mother was a good worker and helped with the household duties such as cooking and minding the babies and, at times, helping with the field work.

The United States entered World War II against Japan after the bombing of Pearl Harbor. At that time, the Civilian Conservation Corps was disbanded. The young men who had been in the CCC now enlisted in the Army and commenced their training for war. Charles Gandy came home from the Corps, immediately enlisted in the service, and was sent to an Army camp in Louisiana for training in the infantry. After completion of training, his unit was shipped out to the southwest Pacific, becoming some of the first troops to land on Guadalcanal at the start of the war with Japan. The Marines were the first to land on the island and Charles's unit, the 31st Infantry Division, was the next. The Marines and the Infantry fought together to clear the island of Japanese soldiers. After the island was cleared of the enemy the 31st Infantry was shipped out to Lae, in New Guinea.

At Lae, they established a base where new units coming to the area would be trained and oriented to jungle warfare. In addition, they developed a good port for the unloading of ships and they were responsible for the safety and security of the entire base area. They provided personnel for the unloading of the ships and the building of base housing for the incoming troops.

The next military mission for the 31st Infantry Division was to spearhead the amphibious assault invasion of Biak Island off the coast of northwestern Dutch New Guinea. This was a difficult operation for the division as the Japanese were well entrenched with guns and mortars hidden in the many coral caves on the island. Within a week, the island air strips had been secured and air traffic could operate from the island to make bombing runs to the Philippine Islands.

The Philippine Islands would be the next big battle location for the Infantry Division for they would join the 6th Army and go in on the amphibious assault landing at Lingayen Gulf. Their mission was to move out south and secure the Clark Field Airbase and then move on into Manila and clear the city of enemy troops. This was some of the hardest fighting that occurred in the retaking of Manila from the Japanese.

Harold Noles joined the Army just as soon as Pearl Harbor was bombed. He was only seventeen years old but his parents signed for him and let him go. His unit was the 5th Infantry Division and they were ready to go overseas just as soon as their replacement fillers were trained. The unit was at Camp Campbell in Kentucky, and they were ready in November of 1942, to enter the war with England. The Division joined an amphibious assault landing group and arrived at

93

Oran, Tunisia, in North Africa, on the 10th of November 1942. The American Second Army Corps had made a simultaneous assault landing on the same day at Casablanca, Tunisia. They would move along the Mediterranean coast and join up with the 5th Infantry Division. These two units moved along the northern coast of Morocco to Bizerte and on to Algiers, arriving there on 4 December 1942.

The war in North Africa was against some of Hitler's best trained veteran troops the Africa Corps, commanded by General Rommel. Harold was fortunate in this first assignment. He had come very close to becoming a casualty but had managed to escape with a minor injury to his right leg. It was enough to earn a Purple Heart Medal but it was not enough to take him out of action. The 5th Division secured the Port of Algiers then moved on to Bizerte where the unit remained until May of 1943. On the 1st of May the Unit moved into Sicily and captured the town of Syracuse by July 1943. Some of the heaviest fighting occurred in the taking of Syracuse, as this was the last stand of the German army before they abandoned the island and moved to the Italian mainland to join the remainder of the German forces there.

Next, the 5th Infantry moved from Sicily to the west coast of Italy, at Palermo, in September 1943. The objective of the Unit was to move on to Rome and capture the city from the German troops. Their first move was to the Rapido River and move on from there to the Monte Cassino, a German stronghold. It would be the hardest fight yet for the enemy had heavily fortified the mountain top and they had the advantage of the high ground overlooking the roads that led to Rome. By the time the 5th Infantry Division had reached Italy, Harold had been promoted to Sergeant in charge of a heavy machine gun squad. He would meet the most dangerous assignment that he had experienced since the war began.

Harold's machine gun squad was one of the units that were assigned the task of scaling the Monte Cassino, then entering the ruined building and routing the Germans that were holed up in the ruins. Just moving up the mountain side and avoiding the hail of fire was dangerous enough but entering the ruins to remove the enemy troops would be disastrous. Harold's squad made it to the outer walls of the building and managed to get inside before being discovered. The squad had lost one man coming up the mountain, and now there were only four men remaining. They arrived just before daybreak for they had spent the night climbing the mountain. Now that they were in the building they had to find a secure place from which to seek out the enemy within the ruins. They did not have long to wait for the Germans found them first. The squad managed to repel them with a few bursts from a sub-machine gun. It became a game of cat and mouse. The squad members each sought out a niche in the ruins to protect themselves but every time they moved, they received a shot from one or more of the enemy troops. The day wore on and more of the men from the 5th managed to get to the ruins. The arrival of the added help put the Germans on the defensive and Harold and his men were able to dispose of them one by one as they appeared from their hiding spots. Before the day was over Harold's squad had killed seven of the enemy, and only one of his men was wounded seriously enough so that he couldn't continue the fight. The remaining two men and Harold continued fighting until the ruins were captured and the Germans were routed. All of the men in the squad had been wounded at least two or three times during the day and when the fight was over the squad carried their most seriously wounded member down the mountain to the ambulance waiting on the road below to take him to the nearest field hospital.

In addition to another Purple Heart Medal, Harold now was awarded the Silver Star Medal for outstanding heroism in overcoming the enemy and performing a difficult mission under heavy fire. The men in his squad received the Purple Hearts, in addition to Bronze Star Medals for their heroism and their part in the mission.

With the removal of the enemy from Monte Cassino, the roads were clear so the 5th Division could march into Rome with no serious opposition. The Division arrived in Rome on 4 June 1944, where they remained until 15 August 1944. In Rome, the Italian populace gave the Unit a great reception. They were so glad to be rid of the Germans. Stopovers in Rome gave the men of the 5th Division a chance to rest and recuperate from their long struggle from North Africa. It was in Rome that Harold received his promotion to Master Sergeant. He was now a successful soldier who had earned the second highest medal given by the Army for duty above and beyond the call of duty. On 15 August 1944, the 5th Division made an amphibious assault on beaches at Cannes and Toulon in southern France. The mission of the Division was to move inland and north along the Rhone River valley. They joined forces with Patton's armies and moved to the Rhine River. Karlsruhe was a stronghold of some of the German elite troops. They were assigned to protect the city and prevent any enemy forces from crossing into Germany. The 5th Division was to capture the city and secure a crossing of the Rhine at that point giving Allied troops an entry into the homeland of Germany.

They did cross the river and make their quarters in the Schwarz Wald Kaserne where the elite German troops had been quartered. Before the year was out, the war was over and peace in Europe had been declared. Harold and his Unit were on their way back home to the United States. They remained in the service after 90 days of rest and recuperation. They, then, had to stand by, in case they were needed in the Pacific Theater. It turned out they were able to stay in the United States.

Harold remained in the Army and finished out 20 years. He retired to a small town in Central Alabama. Rufus and Lucy moved to Selma after the war and found a small place with their youngest daughter, Diana, who had become a nurse during the war and now worked in the local hospital. She had never married and she would take care of her mother and father. Both of her parents were now disabled, her mother from hard, tiring work all her life and her father from heart trouble, inactivity and obesity. William came home from the war a wounded veteran and was now living on a pension from the government.

The eldest son of the Noles family was Robert William. His father saw to it that his eldest would not go to war during the First World War. At first, when the draft was started, he requested a deferment for him, saying he was needed to manage the farm but this did not work with the Draft Board. He claimed his son was the chief foreman of his field crews, with duties requiring skill and training. He could not easily be replaced. Nevertheless, the Board did not see fit to grant an exemption in his case. This did not stop his father's efforts to prevent his eldest son from going to war.

Next, Robert William was going to the doctor regularly and each time he complained of chest congestion, spells of chills and fever, aches, pains, and general malaise. A solid medical case was made and the doctor suggested that Robert William should be sent to Hot Springs, Arkansas, to "take the waters" for a cure. He was promptly sent to Hot Springs and the Board was notified of the doctor's decision. After a few months, he returned home and this ended any possibility of his entering the military service.

Author's Note: Isn't it strange how Arkansas has played a part in supporting two draft dodgers in two different wars just 50 years apart?

When Robert William returned from his hiatus in Arkansas he married a young lady, Nelda Cooper, from one of the "first settler" families. She lived across the creek along the railroad tracks south of the small town of Fairview, a station stop on the Mobile and Ohio railroad. The town consisted of two general stores, one on each side of the railroad tracks. There was also a cotton gin and a post office. This was a farming community made up of small subsistence farms of forty to sixty acres. The staple crops were cotton, corn, peanuts and a large garden plot. Most of the farmers kept cows for milk and butter and hogs for meat and lard.

The new in-laws of Robert William provided him and his wife with a house and forty acres of land which he could tend as a sharecropper. His in-laws also provided the necessaries for making a crop and he provided the labor and expertise. Both parties shared in the worth of the crop at harvest, however the landlord was paid first, then the sharecropper got his share, if any remained. Many years, little was left for the farmer and most years this was the case for Robert William. It seemed he could boss workers but he was not too good at doing the work himself.

After a few years at hit or miss sharecropping, he decided to seek another means of providing for his growing family. He convinced one of the bankers at the county seat to loan him enough money to open a general store in the town of Fairview. It was the third general store in Fairview and he would be in competition with the two stores that had seen him through several lean years when he was sharecropping. The new store was built, stocked with all the necessary items, and opened for business in time for the start of the new farming year. Many of the first customers were those who had been dealing with one or both of the other stores. In fact, most of the new customers had debts outstanding at the other stores, yet Robert William extended more credit for the new crop year. It turned out that his first year in business was a good crop year and most of his debtors were able to pay most of what was owed him. He was able to make his loan payment to the bank and keep his business insurance paid in full. The second business year was not so good for crops were short and the price of cotton was down and the new store struggled through the summer and fall. After the crops were gathered and the cotton sold, less than half of the debtors were able to pay out for the year.

Winter set in and folks were not buying anything and all that Robert William and his clerk had to do was sit by the pot belly stove, stay warm and wait for a customer with some cash. It was obvious that something had to be done and to become bankrupt was out of the question for only crooks went that way.

The weather was cold that night and the temperature was supposed to be down to zero. He and the clerk decided both heaters should be filled with coal and banked for the night. Around two o'clock in the morning, someone looked out and saw the red glow in the area of the store. By the time anyone could get there, the building was engulfed in flames. Just as Robert William got to the store the heat and flames had reached the kerosene tank. It exploded and spread the flames over the entire building. A careful inspection, after the ashes had cooled, showed nothing of value remained of the store or its contents.

The people of the community were shocked for never before had a store burned in the area. What went wrong? Was it due to carelessness on the part of Robert William or maybe his clerk? Fortunately the insurance on the store and contents was paid up and he had no losses. The insurance paid all of the outstanding indebtedness for supplies and paid off the bank loans. Some folks seemed to think he made out all right and that he came out smelling like a rose. Could the store have been "accidentally-on-purpose" fired for the insurance money, surely not, for Robert William was honest and a pillar of the community. But some remembered when he got sickly just in time to avoid the draft but was that dishonest? It was only a bit of strategy to avoid becoming "cannon fodder" in the trenches of the Ardennes Forest in France.

As soon as all the debts were paid to the bank, Robert William commenced to plan the rebuilding of the store. This time he had money to rebuild and no bank loan was needed. He built a larger and better store. By early spring he was in business again and extending credit to old customers. Two years later the new store burned one mid-December night. The weather was bitter cold and there was snow on the ground. The high winds drifted the snow across the landscape all night. Again the store and stock were a total loss, and again the insurance was paid in full and it was said later that William received an ample settlement from the insurance company.

Could this second burning have just been a coincidence? It was strange though that these were the only store burning in this area for many years. Would an arsonist have chosen to just burn Robert William's stores and no others? The second burning convinced most of the community that he may have had something to do with the destruction of the two stores for his personal fortune seemed to increase each time he settled his insurance claims. The second store burning ended his efforts as a store owner.

Now that he had money in the bank, he bought the forty acres and the house he had been renting from his in-laws. His family had grown and consisted of three boys and two girls. The farm could now be rented out on shares and he could seek a more suitable endeavor for himself.

The Postmaster job became available and he was hired for the position. In addition to his salary, he made money by leasing one of his buildings to the government to house the post office. While he was in business, he learned his lessons well. He now knew how to milk the goat, so to speak. A weekly insurance route came open for the area for which he secured the contract and turned it over to his oldest son to operate.

Robert William was on easy street, you might say, for things were going his way at last. Each year he would buy himself a new blue serge suit, and he was now a deacon of the church. He had a large gold watch with a heavy gold chain which was always prominently displayed across the front of his vest. He drove a new Chevrolet car and was thought of as a successful member of the community. Robert William ruled his family with an "iron hand". They were required to respond to his every beck and call. The meals were served on time and no one was allowed to touch a thing until he said the blessing. To cross him meant sure and dire punishment, usually with a peach switch or a razor strop. His oldest son was told he would service the weekly insurance route collections, no ifs, ands, or buts about it. The son had no choice. The two girls were told what they would and wouldn't do and consequently when they graduated from high school, they promptly got married and moved as far as they could from their father. The oldest girl married her high school sweetheart and they moved to Birmingham. She had always wanted to become a nurse and now she had the opportunity for her husband had a good job and he could afford to send her to nursing school right there in Birmingham. After two years of nurses training, she graduated and found a position in one of the local hospitals. Now the two of them could afford to have a home of their own. They were destined not to have many years together as she contracted tuberculosis. Three years to the day, after graduating from nursing school, she passed away.

The younger girl married one of the young men who attended the family church. They were married after they graduated from high school and moved to Tennessee, where he attended the seminary. She found work as a stenographer and her salary helped to pay for his training at the seminary. Within two years, he graduated and was ordained as a minister of the gospel. His first church assignment was in Tennessee. He remained there for twenty years at the same church and it was there they raised their family of four children.

About the time the girls left home, it was obvious that the country would go to war and Robert William had no intention of allowing his oldest son to go to war. He set about getting a position on the local draft board. This just might give him an advantage to prevent his son Henry from serving in the military service during the conflict with Japan. Since young married men with children usually got a low induction number, he saw to it that Henry married right away.

Henry's wife-to-be was a young widow with two small children whom his father had picked for him. Now Henry was a legitimate family man. Then there was the other source for a possible deferment. He would have Henry report regularly to see the family doctor and he was to complain of chest pains and asthma. Surely this would get him deferred if he were to be called.

The war came and things changed but the "iron hand" control of his family did not soften. In fact, it became more rigid after the two girls married and moved away from his sphere of influence over their lives. Henry was always at his side, doing his every wish. The boy had become completely subdued by the will of his father. He would never be able to think for himself, for what little spirit he once had was now gone. He would be a slave to his father as long as they both lived.

The two younger sons Sam and Pat were to severely test their father's mettle. They were rogues, incorrigible teenagers. Punishment only fortified their determination to succeed in having their own way. In high school they learned to smoke cigarettes and of course this brought on severe punishment but they continued to slip around and smoke. Their next evil influence was drinking beer and hanging out at juke joints. This brought more punishment, restrictions and more vicious tirades from their father concerning their evil ways. At this point Sam and Pat resolved to obtain funds any way they could to pay their way as they were determined to leave home for good.

Misfortune provided a chance for the boys to meet an older man, a petty thief, who wished to go big time and needed some young blood to help him rob some stores and banks. Here were two eager would-be bank robbers ready to play their part for a cut of the loot. It seemed Sam and Pat had found a readymade solution to their money problems. The job was planned. The older man knew where to steal an automobile, the boys stole it and they were on their way. Their first job was a small bank in a sleepy little town in northern part of the State. Sam drove the car, Pat stood guard at the door and the older man shoved a gun in the teller's face. They made it back to the car with the money and got out of town fast, headed north. Their success did not last. Ten miles away they were taken into custody by a sheriff's posse at a road block.

Two days later, Robert William was notified that Sam and Pat were in jail charged with bank robbery, auto theft and grand larceny. Three months later the trial was held and the two boys were given two years in jail since they were under twenty-one and it was their first offense. With their father's influence and the fact that the country was at war with Japan and Germany and needed every young man it could get in a uniform, the judge gave them probation if they would immediately enlist in the Army for early shipment to the battle front. Both of the boys enlisted the following day.

Robert William was devastated. He had failed. First the girls were gone and now the two young sons were gone. The boys had besmirched the family's good name and since they were to be assigned to the front lines, he would probably never see them again. All he had remaining was Henry, good faithful Henry, a son who looked up to him. As long as Robert William lived, he could never understand why his children turned out as they did. Why didn't they love him? He lived a long life, and then had a stroke that put him in a coma. After five years in a coma he passed away. His faithful wife and loving son Henry tended to him daily for the five years.

102

Now we will find out how the two younger boys made out in life. Yes, Henry did receive his draft call for induction into the Army, but he failed the physical and was sent home as a 4-F. He was still collecting his weekly insurance route the day that he left this world. The two young renegades Sam and Pat were tough, determined, and they knew where they were going and how to get there. After all they did figure out a way, such as it was, to get away from their domineering father. The boys, having enlisted in the Army at the judge's "request" received their military training at Fort McClelland, Alabama. After completing military training, they were shipped out to England as infantry replacements. They joined a Regimental Combat Team whose destiny was to hit the beaches at Normandy, France, on D-Day, H-hour on 6 June 1944. They survived the first day in hell and fought through the hedgerows of Normandy. Their Combat Infantry Team joined General George Patton's 3rd Army. They moved through the Alsace area and on to participate in the Battle of the Bulge. At the crossing of the Rhine River at Remagen, Germany, they were some of the first troops to enter Germany before the bridge over the Rhine River was destroyed by the Germans. The Germans finally managed to destroy the bridge after nine days. By the time the bridge was destroyed, two pontoon bridges had been built and they provided a crossing from Remagen to Epperley, on the north side of the river. Both Sam and Pat had been wounded and had received the Purple Heart Medal but their wounds were not serious enough to keep them out of combat. They remained with the 3rd Army to the end of the war and their Unit was in Mannheim, Germany, when peace was declared. After the war they remained in the service and saw duty in the Occupation Forces in Japan.

When the Korean War began they were shipped out to Korea in the first contingent of troops and they remained there until the peace was declared. They stayed in the Army for twenty years and retired. The last anyone ever heard from them they were basking in the sun on the beaches in South Texas.

Did all of this begin when Robert William planned his way to prevent being drafted during World War I? Were the store burnings perpetrated by him or were they really just acts of chance? What drove him to the fanatic control of his children? Some would assume that since he got away with deceiving the draft board in his early years that it gave him the courage to do as he pleased the remainder of his life. If he did indeed orchestrate the burning of the stores and then deceived the insurance companies and got away with it, surely he must have felt that he was capable of doing anything that he wished to do.

In the small town of Fairview, there were two general stores. They had been there since the turn of the century. Now and again a third store would come into being for a short time and it would either close for lack of business or mysteriously burn on a dark cold moonless night. The oldest store was east of the railroad track opposite the railway depot and was owned by the Callaway family.

As you walked up the steps and through the big double doors, ahead in the center of the store stood a large cast iron coal-burning heater. To the left and to the right were glass showcases extending the length of the store building. Behind the cases, along the walls from the floor to the ceiling grocery items and dry goods were stocked. The rear of the store contained a large storage room where items such as fertilizer, plows, farm tools and other bulky items were stored. Out front there was a single hand-operated gasoline pump and a kerosene tank for dispensing coal oil. The kerosene cost a nickel a gallon and it was used to fill lamps in the homes. To prevent the oil from being spilled out of the small pouring nozzle of the oil can while it was being taken home, there was always a bucket of small Irish potatoes sitting near the oil tank. One of the potatoes would be pushed down over the nozzle on the oil can to prevent it from leaking.

A Country Store

    The store owner was something of a banker or you might say a pawn broker. Sharecroppers would come to him and hock their souls and their coming crops in order to borrow money for fertilizer, seed, tools and food staples until their crops were harvested. Many times the loan from the store owner would not amount to over a hundred dollars for there was not much the sharecropper required for the "year's run". At times it would be necessary for the borrower to add a few necessaries such as a pair of brogans for work in the fields. The children would go barefooted all summer so they didn't require shoes except a "Sunday-go-to-meeting" pair.

    In the 1920s, country stores were seldom robbed but after the bank failures in the 1930s, bank robbing became a popular way for thieves to get money. They felt it was a way to get even with the bankers since they had closed their doors and deliberately taken the people's money. Bank robbing was an every week affair in the thirties. Then there was a rise in the robbing of country stores by the petty thieves. They didn't get much money but the risk was minimal for hardly ever was there a guard or law officer anywhere near the store. To reduce the robbing of some stores the owners would use a vicious guard dog in the store at night and others would rig set guns with trip wires. The set guns rigged with trip wire were dangerous even for the owners, for some store owners had been known to have gotten shot by their own guns. The days of the Great Depression in the 1930s were a most trying time for people in Central Alabama.

Clayton Noles was the third child and second son of Richard Noles and his wife, Amanda. He was a likely young man when he was growing up on his father's farm and he did his share of the work while he was there. His older brother seemed to be his father's favorite but that didn't seem to bother him as it was natural in old southern families. The eldest son was usually coached and trained to be his father's successor.

The only unusual thing that happened to Clayton was as a teenager he was bitten by a timber rattler which almost took his life. It took two years for Clayton to recuperate from the snake bite. In his early twenties, he married Lois Walker, a girl he had known all of his life. She was the oldest daughter of the family that lived in the big house just across the creek from the Noles farm.

Their family grew as the years passed by. There were two girls and the baby of the family was a boy. After Clayton married, he left home, for the family farm had been foreclosed and it was time for him to move on. He found a job working in Public Works. He was glad to leave the farm. He had never liked farm work. The failure of the jobs in the public sector after the fall of the stock market and the closing of the banks forced him and his family to work as sharecroppers for three years before he could find other work. In the early 1930s, after the bank closings, he found work with a pipe laying company that was building the "big inch" gas transmission line. The line was being laid from the gas fields in Louisiana, to Washington D.C. In the future, more pipes would be laid along this same pipeline route.

Clayton came home from the job site in the Carolinas to spend a few days with the family over the Fourth of July weekend. He joined some of the friends he grew up with on the morning of the fourth and they started drinking moonshine. His friends were known all over the county for being moonshiners. It was all they had ever done. It seemed that sometime during the afternoon they decided to load up in an old Model T Ford and go for more "shine". Somewhere along one of the gravel country roads later that afternoon Clayton was run over and killed by the Model T. Evidently, all of those in the car were drinking, according to a witness. One member of the party claimed that Clayton climbed out on the fender of the car then fell off and the car wheels ran over him. It would have been quite a feat for a trained stunt man who was cold sober. How could a drunken person perform such an act?

It seemed plausible that a drunk could fall out of the car but to fall under the wheels seemed unlikely. In the investigation each man swore he climbed out and fell under the wheels. But it was later found that there was bad blood between Clayton and the driver of the car over an old debt and some whiskey. Nothing ever came of this development and the case was closed. No one ever believed the story of how he happened to die. They always figured it was a case of murder to settle an old score.

After the funeral, Lois was taken in by and lived with her older brother. Dolly, Clayton and Lois's oldest girl, had finished school and was teaching at the local elementary school and her husband had a small farm in Cahaba, Alabama, where he raised hogs for the market. Daisy, the younger daughter, married the brother of her sister Dolly's husband and they lived on a small farm next to her sister. The two sisters were close and the two families helped each other with their farm work. After Daisy's first child arrived, her mother came to live with her so she could take care of the baby and Daisy could help out with the work on the farm. Their uncle Tom, Lois's older brother would look in on the two families now and then to be sure they were making it alright.

Clayton Junior was taken in by his grandfather and Junior grew up with the help of an uncle and living with his grandparents. He was never serious about school. He played hooky more than he attended class. About the time he started high school, he acquired a taste for whiskey which led to a tendency to start fights with anyone at any time he got the urge to do so. By the time he reached eighteen years of age he was incorrigible and no one could control him.

He had an idea that he wanted to join the Marine Corps and go to war since the war had just begun. His grandfather agreed with him and decided it would be best for him to join the military. It might straighten him out and make a man of him. On his eighteenth birthday he joined the Marines. He didn't last long enough to complete basic training. Junior became the scourge of the Corps, drunk and disorderly, fighting, absent without leave and he showed a gross lack of military discipline. Within six months, he was court marshaled and drummed out of the service.

After discharge, Junior returned to his old haunts and fell in with a crowd of bootleggers from down around Selma. One of the older "shine" merchants had a beautiful blond daughter who had just come of age. Junior fell head over heels in love her. He was told straight out "don't mess with her, she ain't for the likes of you! If you continue to see her you will not live to regret it." Nevertheless, Junior and the girl slipped off and got married.

Just one week to the day after her father found they were married, Junior was found murdered. He was dressed in clothes that had just been freshly laundered, starched and ironed. His stomach had been pumped and they found him lying in a freshly plowed field. It looked as if someone had plowed the field and laid the body down in the fresh plowed ground. There were no marks or tracks leading into or out of the field. It was as if a big bird had flown over, deposited the body and flew on its way.

Junior's grandfather and uncle spent a large sum of money on hiring detectives to work on the case trying to find the murderer. Nothing ever came of the investigations. Most of the people around the area were sure that the girl's father did the dirty deed but there was no proof. It seemed the villain had covered his tracks completely.

Her father was a big bootlegger in the days of prohibition and as such he had the money to buy off the Sheriff. With the help of the paid sheriff he was able to squash any of the investigations. The fact that Junior was a dishonorably discharged service man made it easy for the Sheriff to look the other way for a friend with money. After all the girl's father was mostly responsible for getting the Sheriff elected for it was his liquor and his money that bought the Sheriff most of his votes.

Oh! There was one more item in that mystery. The farm hand that had plowed the field the day before the body was found could not be located. No one knew who he was and he had just vanished. Some said he had gone to California, others said they didn't know anything about his whereabouts. It was obvious the local people would stay quiet if they knew what was good for them.

Days of Prohibition

The twenties and the thirties were the days when our all-knowing, caring political fathers in Washington decreed that, we the people should be protected from the evils of "Demon Rum". They, in their infinite wisdom, saved our poor unenlightened souls by passing a law prohibiting the manufacture, sales or use of intoxicating beverages.

Whiskey-making required large quantities of grain such as corn, or rye and large quantities of sugar. The corn and rye were easily grown but the sugar usually had to be purchased at a store. Many times the purchase of large quantities of sugar would lead the Revenue Officer straight to the whiskey maker. To avoid detection, many of the moonshine makers would buy a small bag of sugar at one store then go to the other stores around the area and buy one bag at each. They would sometimes even go to another county to buy sugar.

The Whiskey Still

There was another source of sugar that was not so easily traced to the whiskey maker and that was cane syrup. Most small farms could produce all of the ingredients needed in the manufacture of illegal whiskey. Normally the still was located in dense woods near a small creek where plenty of clean water was available. The grain, sugar and water were mixed in barrels and set up to ferment. Then the liquid from these barrels was distilled.

The whiskey was stored in oak kegs that had been charred inside and this gave the moonshine a color similar to store-bought bourbon. Charring the oak kegs and aging the moonshine was also thought to take out some of the harshness of the "white lightning". Alcohol content of the whiskey was about 35%.

The making of moonshine or as the revenue officers referred to it, unlicensed whiskey, probably began in Ireland by the Scotch

Immigrants when the English Crown began to tax the manufacture of whiskey. When the Scotch-Irish began to immigrate to the colonies in the New World, they brought with them the knowledge and the desire to produce good drinking whiskey. After the Revolutionary War, the new nation of the United States was bankrupt from financing the war. Thomas Jefferson began seeking revenue from every source. One of the first new taxes in the early 1790s was an excise tax on the manufacture of whiskey. The whiskey makers refused to pay the tax and the government sent in Army troops to enforce the law and collect taxes. There was an all-out war between them and the tax collectors. This became known as the "Whiskey Rebellion of 1794". The farmers who were making whiskey claimed they were only converting their grain, for which there was no market, into a product that they could sell and it should not be taxed.

Again in the 1870s, the Internal Revenue Commissioner was looking for a greater source of revenue. He felt the taxes that were lost to moonshiner operations would equal the legitimate amount of taxes collected for the whole country. The State of Georgia, in the 1960s, figured the state was losing fifty million dollars every year due to the manufacture and sale of unlicensed whiskey.

Moonshine stills have operated for years from West Virginia, through the Blue Ridge Mountains, The Carolinas, Georgia, Tennessee and Alabama. Even today stills continue to operate in these areas. Many men found whiskey making to be a way of obtaining quick cash and most times if they were caught the penalty was not severe. At first the Federal Agents were the enforcing agency to control the whiskey making. This changed during Prohibition and much of the enforcement of the laws became the responsibility of the local sheriff. Again the enforcement changed and Federal Agents are now in charge of hunting down those that make and sell unlicensed whiskey.

In the old days and during the Depression years the moonshine whiskey makers were proud of their product. They knew it tasted good and more than that, it was safe from poisonous substances such as lead, oils and various other harmful materials. This was a way of converting their corn and rye crops to a product for which there was a ready cash market. The bulk of their customers were regular buyers and this assured them of a constant market for every gallon of whiskey they could produce. Moonshine was usually sold in quart and half gallon fruit jars.

Whiskey makers usually made their own stills from expensive copper sheet metal. They had a pattern that had been handed down for generations that showed how to form each piece of the still. Sheet iron could be used to make the still but it left a bad taste in the finished whiskey. The entire still was made of copper including the copper coil that was used for condensing the steam from the boiler. Some greedy moon shiners would use an old automobile radiator as a condensing coil but this usually poisoned the whiskey with rust and lead from the radiator. Seldom did the moonshiners use the same location for an operation. They would make one run and then move the still to another area for the next run. By moving each time very little of the area around or leading to the still was disturbed or showed signs of being used for a still site. Revenue Officers knew how to look for the signs that indicated a still was in the area. Many times the Officers would follow a small stream for they knew that fresh cool water was needed to make the still operate. Many times the Officers would fly over an area suspected of being a still site to look for smoke from the cooker. The still operator was careful to camouflage the site of his operation both from the ground and from the air. At times the Officers would walk through the suspected area smelling for the scent of souring mash. Many stills were found because informers wanted to get even with someone, maybe a competitor in the same area.

Clara Noles was the second daughter and the fourth child of the Noles family. She married Thomas Wilson, a young man who was employed by the Mobile and Ohio railroad. Thomas's father was the local school teacher during the week and on Sunday he was the local "Hard Shell Baptist" preacher. Clara was well educated she had finished high school and had a good command of reading, writing and mathematics. Seldom did a young lady get a chance to get more than two or three years of schooling in those days.

The Wilson family did well and saved their money and the second year of their marriage they purchased a small farm with a nice old log house and a good barn. Now they could have a garden, hogs and a cow, as well as chickens. These would provide plenty of food. In the early twenties, 1922, the railroad commenced to lay off workers especially in the construction crews and Thomas was laid off. For the next two years they worked their small farm and were able to make their crops without borrowing money.

Now the family included four children, two girls and two boys. Soon they would need to go to school. Clara knew the school system in their county was one of the poorest in the state and she wanted her children to have a good education. That year the family bought a new Model T Ford with rollup glass windows and the family made a trip to Mobile in the southern corner of the state. They found a place they could rent for $60 per year. This large farm was been abandoned by its northern owner who had returned to his home in Ohio. They rented the farm, went back, loaded up their belongings and moved to Mobile County. They rented their old place to Clara's brother for more than enough to pay the rent on the new place.

The year they moved to Mobile County the schools were consolidated and the school bus routes were put out for bid. Thomas was successful in obtaining the route contract in their area. The successful bidder would furnish the truck chassis, the school board furnished the coach body and the contractor would operate the bus and pay all expenses. It was an annual contract that paid $100 per month. This was a good deal during these troubling times in 1929 just after the fall of the stock market. With the bus contract and the farm the family was able to make a good living, even in those difficult times.

The bus route ran along the highway and picked up children from the small two-room schools and took them to the larger consolidated school. Since there was nothing to do while the children were in school Thomas found a job in the village near the school. He was a good carpenter so he could work during school hours repairing

113

the older homes in the company-owned village. It was a perfect setup and brought in more money for the family.

Thomas was able to renew his contract every year for the school bus and during the years of World War II, he had two contracts. During the war, there was a housing boom going on in the areas which furnished housing for the workers that were moving in to work at the shipyards. Thomas hired drivers for his two buses and started a home-building business. Prior to the war, Mobile was a sleepy seaport town of 90,000. As soon as the war began workers poured into the city.

There were seven shipyards in the harbor and all types of skills were needed. Within the first two year after the bombing of Pearl Harbor the population of the city had swelled to 500,000. Government housing projects were going up all over the city. Even the public golf courses were covered with temporary housing. People were cleaning out their garages and renting them for workers to have a place to sleep. Boarding houses were full and running over with guests. Some of them were renting out the same beds twice each day, once for the worker on the day shift and next for the worker on the night shift. Housing construction was booming but there was still not enough for all the workers to have an adequate place to live.

With the move to the new place, the Wilson children had excellent schools to attend. The consolidation of the school system made it possible for each of the larger schools to have the best of teachers. A new high school had just been completed in the late twenties and it would provide for 2000 students. This was an excellent school facility. It not only had an excellent academic curriculum but there was a well-staffed vocational school included. Many students only attended the vocational school to learn a trade and then enter the work force as an apprentice.

The oldest daughter of the Wilson family finished high school and went on to the state teachers college. After she completed her college training she was employed as a teacher and she taught school for the next thirty five years.

The next child was Walter. After finishing high school he entered a work scholarship program with the state university. He worked one semester and went to school the next semester. He was in his second year at school when World War II began. With his training in engineering he was assigned to the U.S. Army Corps of Engineers. He attended Officers Training School and became a Second Lieutenant. After a year of training he was shipped out to the Southwest Pacific Theater of Operation in a Combat Engineer battalion. His unit first saw action at the amphibious assault at Aitape, in New Guinea.

The Engineer Combat battalion went ashore during the landing with the First Australian Infantry Division and their immediate goal was to capture the Tadji Airstrip being held by the Japanese. As Walter's landing craft was approaching the beach in very rough surf conditions it stopped on a sand bar some 100 yards off the beach. When one of the soldiers was exiting the landing craft he stepped into a deep spot in the surf and went under. Walter was right behind the man and he was able to rescue him and tow him into the beach. For this rescue of a fellow soldier and by saving his life, Walter was awarded the Soldiers Medal.

By the end of the first day of fighting, the airstrip had been secured. Walter's unit was assigned the task of rebuilding the Tadji Airstrip for it had been bombed and was filled with bomb craters. In addition to its damaged condition the airstrip had to be enlarged, widened and lengthened. The Engineer Combat Battalion was given seven days to complete the project and have it ready for operation. Heavy equipment was put to work night and day to clear the area, fill the craters and commence the enlargement of the airstrip. A coral pit was opened to provide the fill material needed for the repairs. The project was nearly finished on the seventh day and shortly after noon an emergency landing of fighter planes were landing on the field just as the last equipment was being removed. For his work in supervising, and directing the rebuilding of the airstrip in record time Walter was awarded the Bronze Star Medal.

After the Aitape campaign was secured the Engineer Combat Battalion's next move was to join the Infantry Unit that was making the Amphibious Assault Landing on Noemfoor Island, in Dutch New

Guinea. On this landing the Engineers were required to go in with the first wave of infantry and use the heavy equipment to build ramps of coral rock out over the shallow reef area. This was necessary in order to get the motor vehicles and guns unloaded over the reefs. The ramps would have to extend for 200 yards out to deep water The first two ramps were completed by the close of the first day. Heavy equipment continued to work through the first night and by the morning of the second day the five ramps needed were complete.

After the island was secured the Engineer Combat Battalion built a road network around the island after they had repaired the airstrip. They remained on the island until they were ordered to move to Morotai Island to wait for a move to the Philippine Islands. Walter's unit joined with elements of the 6th Army and made the assault landing at Lingayen Gulf, a point on the northwest coast of Luzon, just north of Clark Field and Manila. The mission of the Combat Engineer Battalion was to move south to Clark Field, secure the airfield and make repairs to the runways so Allied planes could use the field. On arrival at the field and within the first day they had secured the airfield and made the necessary repairs. Their new mission was to continue to move south to Manila and clear the wreckage and debris from the Port of Manila so that troopships and supplies could be brought in by sea to the city. The docks were repaired and unloading facilities were put in place. While the work was going on at the docks, the infantry was clearing the enemy from Walled City the old Spanish Fortress which was built when the Spanish occupied the Philippine Islands. The engineers provided explosive teams to blast holes in the twenty foot high granite walls in order for the infantry to enter the fortress.

When the war ended the Engineer Combat Battalion was moved to Yokohama on the main island of Japan to repair the port facilities and the road network for the Allied Occupation Troops. After the port was repaired, Walter, who had been promoted to the rank of Captain, was eligible to return to the United States. His trip home was a pleasant one. He secured a berth on the aircraft carrier Intrepid which had been pressed into service as a troop carrier to return troops to the

States. The trip was very nice and he shared a stateroom with a fellow officer. The meals were the best the Navy had and the trip only took eight days to arrive in San Francisco, California.

After the close of the war, he was re-called to active duty and assigned to Europe. His unit was assigned to rebuilding the infrastructure of Germany that was destroyed during the war. Their first project was the rebuilding of the bridges on the Autobahn. After this tour of duty the Korean War broke out and he was shipped to Korea to serve in that conflict. After Korea, he was able to return to civilian life and complete his education. He went on to become a professional engineer.

The second son, Vernon Wilson, finished high school just as the war began and he was employed in the shipyard until he was drafted into the military service. He entered the army and completed his basic training at Camp Edwards, Massachusetts. His unit was sent to England. From there he was with the Patton's 3rd Army. They made the D-Day landing on Omaha Beach in the invasion of Europe in 1944. He was a Sergeant in an Anti-Aircraft Artillery unit attached to the 14th Armored Division. His division saw action throughout France and Germany and they participated in the Battle of the Bulge which was one of the toughest battles of the war. Vernon earned a Bronze Star Medal for his actions during the Battle. It was in this battle that he also earned a Purple Heart Medal. After the war he returned to the States, completed his education, became an electrical engineer. He worked for an electronics manufacturing company that was making parts for the space industry.

The youngest daughter of the Wilson family finished high school just as the war was winding down in the Pacific and she was employed for two years in the Federal Civil Service. After the close of the war and the layoffs that occurred she obtained a scholarship to enter the state university system. She graduated with a bachelor's degree in education and began a teaching assignment. Each summer after school was out for vacation she continued to study for a Master's degree in Education. She continued to teach for the next twenty years.

The Wilson family made a wise choice in moving away from the poorest county in the state and moving to an area where there was employment. Being located in a county with good schools was a real asset for the children so that they were able to get a quality education.

Mavis was the fourth daughter of the Noles family. She married Clarence Trent. Her husband was from a family of early settlers in the area near her father's farm. They had known each other since they were children and everyone thought that one day they would be married. Clarence's grandfather had given him title to an 80 acre farm with a substantial log house and a good barn when he turned twenty one years of age. When Mavis reached eighteen, they were married on her birthday.

Clarence was a good provider. He was a good farmer and always had a successful crop. He was a prudent young man and saved his money so he could finance his crops every year without borrowing and getting into debt with the money lenders. After the crops were harvested and winter set in, he was busy setting his trap lines to catch raccoons, beavers, skunks, foxes and other fur-bearing animals. This was one way he could make some extra money to see them through the winter. All through the Depression years there was a good market for furs and it brought in a good bit of cash for the family.

Their family consisted of one girl and two boys, the girl being the oldest. The boys were too young to be called in the draft when World War II was going on. The children were old enough to work on the farm and Clarence had enough help in the family to do the farm work during those years. With the government subsidy for the cotton and peanut crops the family did well.

The daughter of the family was named Bernice, who married her high school sweetheart Ralph Swan. In July of 1942, Ralph was drafted and sent to Fort Jackson, South Carolina, where he spent six months in basic training. After basic training was completed he was assigned to the Quartermaster Supply Corps. Early in 1943 his battalion was shipped out overseas. The destination for his battalion was Ramgarh, India, in the China-Burma Theater of Operations.

The battalion loaded aboard ship in New Orleans, for the trip to India and the first leg of their journey was through the Gulf of Mexico to the south Atlantic. From there, the ship proceeded around the Cape of Good Hope and South Africa, up the east coast of Africa through the Indian Ocean to Calcutta, India. After unloading in Calcutta they continued by truck to the training center that had been established in early 1942 at Ramgarh, India.

Ralph's Battalion of Quartermaster personnel had their first mission training Chinese soldiers to fight against the Japanese that had invaded Burma and China. Their second mission, after spending six months training Chinese soldiers, was to organize and build fuel lines from Assam to Ledo. The most important mission of the battalion was to organize and provide supplies for the support of the Airlift over the "Hump" across the Himalayan Mountains to China. After the Ledo road was completed to connect Ledo with the Burma Road the Quartermaster Battalion furnished all the trucks and planes with supplies for China. The C-47 cargo planes flew supplies over the "Hump". General Chennault's Flying Tiger fighter planes provided protection from Japanese aircraft for the truck convoys.

The Burma/India area was rough terrain and living conditions in camp were not the best. Ralph came down with malaria after being there for eight months and his chills and fever were very debilitating. After serving in the theater for two years he developed a case of "jungle rot" a skin infection that slowly spread all over his body. He was flown back to the States for treatment at the Veterans Hospital in Nashville, Tennessee. The skin infection took two years to clear up and Ralph spent the entire time in the hospital.

The war ended and Ralph was still in the hospital. He was not discharged until the summer of 1946. When he was discharged the Army gave him a 50% disability pension for he would never be able to overcome the infection of the jungle rot. He and his wife returned to the old home place and built their house on a five acre plot down below the old house near the lower end of the peach orchard.

After he returned from service in the war through the funds provided by the G.I. Bill, Ralph was able to attend the state university where he received a degree in education. He was hired by the local school board to teach in the local elementary school and he remained a school teacher the rest of his life.

The oldest son, Tyron, finished high school and entered the Merchant Marines and commenced training as a Cadet. His first trip at sea was in a merchant ship convoy carrying war supplies through the North Atlantic to Murmansk, Russia. While his convoy was traveling in the North Atlantic four of the merchant ships were torpedoed by German submarines. Those days in the Atlantic were very dangerous and many ships were lost to submarine warfare. On his third trip in convoy in the North Atlantic his ship was torpedoed and he and most of his crew were rescued by one of the other ships in the convoy.

When Tyron returned to the States, he was granted two weeks leave before he signed on another merchant ship. On his new ship he would leave out of New Orleans, go through the Panama Canal and proceed to Australia with war supplies for the American troops in that area. After his ship returned to the States at San Francisco, it was loaded with ammunition, bombs and war materiel and on this trip their destination was Lae, New Guinea. Over a period of five years he had become an Able Seaman and was studying to become a First Mate. After ten years of service he became a First Mate and was spending all of his time at sea. He spent twenty years at sea and then retired back home to his father's farm.

The younger son, Ira, joined the Army Air Force after the war was over and became a member of an air crew on a bomber. He had just gotten in the service and completed his basic training when the Korean War began. His bomber unit was one of the first units of the Air Corps to be deployed to Korea. After a year of bombing runs over North Korea he had become a veteran machine gunner.

When the war was over his bomber unit was deployed back to the States. Upon returning home with his unit to the States he requested to be assigned to a school section where men were being trained to service the new electronic guided missile weapons. He spent four years in the missile guidance school and when he graduated he was assigned to a fighter squadron. There he became a member of the crew that installed the new weapons on the planes. He spent twenty years in the service and retired as a Master Sergeant.

When the two sons retired they both went back to the family farm and operated it for their mother. Their father had passed away from a heart attack just a few years before they retired. The boys lived at the old place and took care of their mother for the remainder of her life. Their older sister Bernice and her husband Ralph had retired and they lived just down the road below the peach orchard.

Lydia Noles was the sixth child and the fifth daughter of the family and she married a young man by the name of Herbert Wallace. No one thought the marriage would last for Herbert was sort of the wild type and he did things his way. He had "cut down" his Model T Ford and made a hot rod racer out it and he had installed a cut-out on the exhaust so that everyone would know who was coming down the road. There were some good qualities about the boy. He would work and he had a good job. His job was as a manager of timber land down in Choctaw County along the Alabama River. The property belonged to one of the Congressmen from the state and in addition to being timber land it was also a hunting reserve for he and his Washington friends.

The job paid thirty dollars per month and a five room house was furnished free of rent in the little town of Sunflower. He was required to maintain constant surveillance of the 10,000 acres of river land and keep out unauthorized hunters. This was a natural for Herbert, and a fine horse was provided for transportation through the forest so he could saddle up and survey the property. Another requirement was that the overseer would plant several patches of corn so there would be plenty of bait food for the deer when hunting season began. Food patches for the wild turkeys was also to be provided so that turkey hunting would be good for the guests visiting the reserve.

Herbert was allowed to provide his family with as much wild game as they needed to supplement their food needs. He was at liberty to take as many deer as needed, wild hogs were plentiful to supply their need for pork and there were plenty of wild turkeys. Foraging on the wildlife of the area provided a great deal of the food for the family.

There was a small barn on the property where they could keep a cow if they wished. Fishing in the lakes, sloughs and river were another source of food that was there just for the taking. To Herbert this was almost paradise.

There was a large hunting lodge located on the property down by the river. The lodge was for the visiting dignitaries that the Congressman would invite from Washington. The lodge was not one of Herbert's responsibilities for another family lived at the lodge and maintained it in readiness for the Congressman and his guests. That family did the cooking, served the meals, did the bar-be-cueing and maintained the guest quarters. Herbert's responsibility when the guests arrived was as a hunting party guide. He knew where all the game was and he placed the guests in locations where they could have a trophy hunt every time.

All through the Depression years of the 30s, the Wallace family grew in size. The family consisted of five boys none of whom would be old enough to be in the draft for military service in World War II.

Very soon after the end of World War II eighteen wheel over-the-road truck units were competing with the railroads as freight haulers across the nation. The oldest Wallace son saw the need and purchased a used Peterbilt prime mover and went into business. Markets for his services with the truck came from hauling refrigerated produce from the vegetable farms in Florida to the markets in New York. He was soon able to help his next older brother buy a used Freightliner so that he could get in the trucking business, also.

Business for the trucks continued to improve. The railroads were cutting back on some of their unprofitable lines and the trucks were filling in the void left by the rail closings in post-war years. This situation gave rise to a greater need for eighteen wheel trucks for delivery to the small town abandoned by the rail lines.

The two older brothers were doing so well in the business, that they were able to help their next younger brother purchase a used Peterbilt, so that he, too, could go into business as a truck owner. Now the three brothers could serve most of the markets. The younger brother served the Chicago area bringing in vegetables from the South.

The three brothers and their three trucks were staying busy just delivering vegetables. Eventually, the three brothers helped their fourth brother purchase his truck and go into business. The last brother would find a market for his hauling service by transporting fruit and vegetables from south Texas.

The trucking business for the four boys was coming along well. They were staying busy all the time. As soon as one load was completed, another was waiting to be loaded and delivered. After a few years on the road the eldest brother developed arthritis in his back and shoulders. Since he had been driving for ten years, he felt that he would have to retire. He moved to Mobile and opened a truck repair shop so that he would be in a position to maintain and repair his brothers' trucks and he would lease out his truck. This was the best thing for him. He had an income from the rental of his truck as well as from the shop. Many of his old friends and fellow truck owners brought in their rigs for servicing and repair and his shop stayed full of work all the time.

The fourth brother, who was hauling fruit from Texas, married a young lady from a town near Dallas. After their marriage, they moved to Texas and established their business there along with his brother-in-law who was also a truck owner and cross-country hauler. His wife was also a trained, experienced and licensed truck driver and she drove with him full time. Soon they were able to branch out and purchase another truck, so they each had one.

They expanded their hauling area to California hauling fruit and vegetables from the West Coast farms to the eastern markets. Their fleet had one refrigerator truck so they could handle cut flowers from the flower farms on the west coast. He, his wife and his brother-in-law had a booming business and were staying on the road with a load of produce or flowers every day.

The fifth son did not want any part of the tucking business and after he graduated from high school he got a job in an independent grocery store, learning to become a store manager. It was the kind of work he was interested in, and he wanted to, one day, have a store of his own. He did well for the first two years spending most of his waking hours working. Then he decided to get married. At first he thought it was his idea to get married, but, as time would tell, he found that he had been talked into the union.

She was a beautiful young woman but, as he was to discover later, she was very domineering and possessive. After they were married, she became jealous of the time he was spending at the store. She wanted to know why he didn't spend more time with her, why was he staying late at the store to count inventory and was this all that was going on when he was away from home for more than eight hours each day. His wife was to become a real problem for him and his work. He finally got a divorce and went back to staying with the store full time.

Herbert and Lydia lived on the hunting reserve of the Congressman until the war with Japan began, then they moved to the outskirts of Mobile. He applied for and was accepted at the Chickasaw Shipyard as a night guard at the main gate. It was the type of employment that was well suited for Herbert. It was a bit confining but also rewarding.

He stayed with the shipyard until it closed shortly after the end of the hostilities in the Pacific. He retired to a small place just north of town but he didn't live very long for he had developed a lung problem after many years of smoking. The asthma and lung problems persisted for two or three years and he passed away while he was in his early sixties.

Patrick, Lester and Clyde were the three youngest of the Noles children. When Patrick was a young teenager he learned to drive an automobile and he became his father's chauffeur, for his father had never learned to drive. Besides, his father only had one good eye. Early in life he had lost an eye while clearing land for farming. Richard Noles bought a new Chevrolet sedan and a one and a half ton Chevrolet truck in the mid-twenties as soon as Patrick had reached the age when he could drive a vehicle. Prior to the purchase of the automobile the family had depended on two-horse "surrey with fringe on the top" for family transportation.

Patrick married his long time sweetheart, Ruth, a neighbor's daughter that lived on the next farm up the hill. They moved in with

Patrick's mother and father. These two stayed with his parents and took care of them in their old age. Patrick farmed the two hundred acres and managed the peach farm for his father. Ruth did the cooking, housekeeping, laundry and the management of the household for Patrick's mother. It was an ideal situation for everyone.

There was another member in the household of the old folks for their son Lester had polio when he was six years old and was almost a complete cripple. He had lived with his mother and father all his life. Now Patrick and his wife would care for him, too, along with the parents. Ruth would wash him up in the mornings, help him get dressed, and help him to the table for his meals. She cared for him as if he were her own son. Ruth was a very caring person who took her duties in stride and cared for the whole family as if she had always been a part of it.

When Patrick's parents passed away, he inherited the farm and the responsibility for keeping his afflicted brother which he and Ruth were glad to do. In addition to caring for Patrick's mother and father and caring for Lester, they had their own family of four children. The situation gave Ruth a full load of daily responsibilities. Patrick had his work cut out for him, also, to produce enough food and money to support everyone. But the family made a good living for the whole group and never complained that the job was too hard.

Clyde was the youngest of the Noles family. He was busy at the barn one day, when he was ten, caring for the horses and the mules. One of the mules kicked him in the head and caused him to have a serious concussion. After he spent two years in the hospital, he remained disabled from the accident and was not able take care of himself. The family doctor felt it would be best for him to be placed in an institution where he would be cared for and where medical attention was available on a daily basis. He suffered in the institution for five years. He was getting worse and there was no hope of him recovering. Finally, he passed away as a result of his injuries. It was a dreadful thing to happen to the family for their youngest to go this way. His parents were never able to get over the tragedy.

This is the story of a family that had it all going for them as the Great Depression approached. They persevered through the loss of a fortune and were able to overcome and live out a good and rewarding life. Life was never easy for them but they were willing and able to meet the challenges every day. The Noles were a couple whose children were successful and most of whom produced families of outstanding worth to the country.

By comparing the lives of these three families it is possible to get a look at a cross-section of the people of the times and how they succeeded during troublesome years.

Chapter Six

The Barnes Family

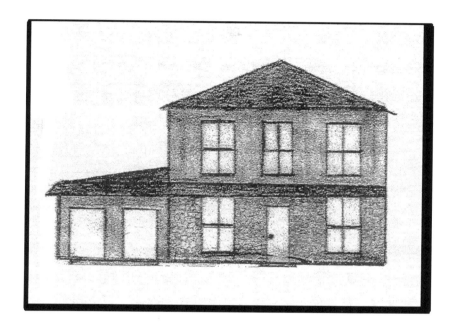

Rudolph Barnes and his wife Estelle had it made. Rudolph's father lived with the family in the large stone house that was built around 1900. A beautiful home set on several acres of pasture land on the state highway, not too many miles north of the port city.

The elder Barnes had been a sawmill owner just after the turn of the century when virgin timber was in demand all over the world. Their home was set near the virgin yellow pine forests where the timber was harvested then shipped by rail to the port. A large sawmill was set near the River on a high bluff where the original settlement of the area was located. After the stands of virgin timber had been depleted, the new enterprise for the family was merchandising. In the years just preceding World War I there was a good market for food products and hardware. The family stores were located in the port city. Rudolph was the oldest child and he was educated as a civil engineer. The second son Thomas was an accountant he managed his father's finances. He was a confirmed bachelor and dedicated all his time and efforts to the family businesses. Estelle, Rudolph's wife, was a medical doctor and a member of the staff of one of the nearby hospitals. In addition to her practice, she stayed busy on the weekends around the community taking care of neighbors and indigents when needed, especially during the Depression.

There was never a time during the Depression that there was not a full time salary for the family each month. In addition to the salary from Estelle's employment, there was income from the food and hardware stores after the war began in Europe in the late thirties.

Rudolph and Estelle had four children, two boys and two girls. The two younger children were still in high school during the war years. In 1940, things were looking good for the family industries for the Barnes' businesses were operating at full capacity. Now people had jobs as employment improved and they could afford to buy groceries and hardware when needed.

Olson Barnes, the oldest son, qualified for a scholarship at the state university, where he began his studies in the autumn of 1940. In the spring of 1941, he was given the opportunity to enter the naval flight training school if he qualified. He started training as an air cadet and early in 1943; he graduated as a naval aviator and was commissioned as an Ensign. His first assignment was as a Catalina PBY seaplane pilot, stationed in Alaska. His unit was charged with the responsibility of surveillance along the coast of Alaska and Canada for the presence of enemy submarines. As the war gained momentum in the Southwest Pacific, his unit was shipped out to Lae on the northeast coast of Papua, New Guinea. Their assignment was night patrol duty along the coast of New Guinea, looking for enemy ships.

128

On one of Olson's recon mission along the northwestern tip of the New Guinea, he was flying over the Birds Head when a Japanese shore battery fired on his plane causing him to ditch in the ocean just before reaching land. His radio man called for a rescue team that was available at Noemfoor Island just a two hour trip east of their location. The plane was in a difficult spot, for with a change of the tide the plane could be drifting onto the shore. The Air Rescue Team arrived in time, took the crew aboard the ship and commenced to tow the Catalina behind the rescue ship. This made for slow travel but after four hours the rescue ship had brought the crew and the plane to safety. They pulled the plane up on the beach and the crews from the airbase came and salvaged it. Olson and his crew were flown back to their base at Lae.

As the war progressed further up the coast of New Guinea, Olson's unit moved to Morotai Island, a small atoll in the South Philippine Sea where they were assigned duty of coastal surveillance along the south of the island of Mindanao, then over to the Princess Palawan Islands and along the northern coast of North Borneo. On one of these coastal surveillance missions Olson and his crew were told to go in to a small atoll just off the northeast coast of British Borneo near the port of Klandasan and pick up two prisoners of war. They were two British officers who had escaped from the Japanese prisoner of war camp located in the area, and which was still held by the Japanese. The prisoner of war camp held Australian and the British servicemen that were captured at Singapore at the beginning of the war. It was Olson and his crew's duty to slip in to the atoll, pick up the two escapees and bring them back to Morotai Island. The plane managed to land in the surf on the north side of the island. A rubber dinghy was launched from the plane and it moved in to shore with two crew members. As soon as the dinghy hit the beach, the two prisoners saw it and made a run for the boat. They jumped in and the dinghy headed for the plane. Before they reached the plane, Japanese soldiers on the atoll saw what was occurring and commenced to fire at the plane and the dinghy. Fortunately they were poor shots and no damage was done. For this daring rescue mission, Olson was awarded the Distinguished Service Medal.

His squadron's last assignment was surveillance of the convoy landing force of 245 ships that were making the last amphibious beachhead assault at Balikpapan, Borneo. They kept a constant lookout for enemy submarines and naval craft along the convoy route from Morotai Island to Balikpapan. The convoy traveled five days at sea before reaching Borneo. When the Catalinas attempted to land after the invasion on the beaches at Balikpapan, the water was so rough that many of the planes were lost or severely damaged in the surf. Since the war was almost over the pilots and crews of the unit were sent home to the States. The war ended in August of 1945, and Olson was taken off active duty. During his war service, he was promoted to Lieutenant Commander. He returned to the university to complete his degree in engineering.

Marian Barnes, the oldest daughter, attended a New England university and graduated with a degree in Fine Arts. She was privileged to stay on, after graduating, to continue her studies and obtain her Master's Degree. Upon completion of her graduate work, she returned to the family home and established an art studio.

She had become a talented artist over the years, skilled in the use of both oil and watercolor. In addition to selling art and arranging monthly showings for other local artists, she developed an excellent retail business selling art supplies and fine art objects.

As her art became known throughout the area, customers from all over the South came to view and purchase her beautiful landscape paintings. She also was sought-after as a portrait painter. She was in business about a year when it became necessary for her to hire two young ladies to manage the sales, so she could devote all of her time to painting. The second year, her profits from the shop showed a dramatic increase. Monthly showings by local artists became a real success. Many beginning artists and some of the older, established artists were showing regularly at her gallery.

For Marian, this was the fulfillment of her fondest dream. She had always wanted to become an accomplished artist. Now with several years' experience in developing her art and the success of her business in sales, she felt she had arrived in the world that she loved.

The second daughter, Janis, chose to be a chemist and seek a position with a local commercial firm. She attended the state university and received her degree in chemistry and then remained to finish a Master Degree. When she graduated she was able to get a position with a local chemical wholesale house in the city. Within her first year on the job she married her sweet heart of long standing and they bought a home in Azalea Place on the west side of the city,

Thaddeus, the youngest of the Rudolph Barnes family, grew up during the World War II years, graduated from high school just at the end of the war, and was fortunate to get a scholarship from the state power company. The company paid his tuition at Auburn University where he received his degree in electrical engineering. His obligation was that he would work for the company for at least five years.

Thaddeus graduated from college in May, 1950, and while in school he had been a member of the Reserve Officers Training Corps. Upon graduation, he received his commission as a Second Lieutenant in the Army, just as the war in Korea broke out. He was called to report for active duty but he did not wish to be a foot soldier, so he applied for flight training in the Air Corps. After a year of training, he was assigned as the co-pilot of a B-24 bomber and joined a bomber group in Korea.

Bombing runs over North Korea were dangerous missions since the Russians were providing the North Koreans and the Red Chinese with MIG 16 fighter planes. Many of the Russian fighters were flown by experienced Russian pilots. On the first bombing run over North Korea, Thaddeus's plane was shot up but they managed to complete the bomb run and make it back to base. They only had two casualties from the strafing. The pilot received some shrapnel in his left arm and shoulder, and one of the gunners was wounded.

Since the pilot was wounded on the first bomb run, Thaddeus was moved into his position. He was assigned a co-pilot who had just arrived from the States. The crew managed to make fifteen more bombing raids into enemy territory before they were attacked again.

This time the damage was done by ground fire from North Korean anti-aircraft artillery, causing damage to the rear of the fuselage, the outboard starboard engine and the bomb bay. They were fortunate enough to be able to make it back to home base with the protection of the accompanying fighter planes.

The crew now had three members including Thaddeus, who were wounded and needed hospital care. Those three were flown to Tokyo, Japan, to the main hospital for surgery and recuperation. All three crew members were air-lifted back to the United States. Their tour of duty was over and they could be discharged as soon as they were physically able. Now Thaddeus could begin his work with the power company

His five year obligation to the company lasted for thirty years until he retired. While working with the company engineering team, he was a part of the steam power generation design team for five years. He showed by his work ethic that he was a dedicated employee, so the company sent him back to the university to get his master's degree in mechanical engineering. When he returned to work he was assigned to the Savannah River nuclear power plant where he was an inspector on the construction of the nuclear reactor. After twenty years in engineering design and construction supervision, he was assigned to the Birmingham office where he handled customer relations for the area until he retired.

Chapter Seven

The Sam Hairston Family

    Sam and Susie Hairston were born before World War I in 1912. Their parents were sharecroppers on a large cotton farm in Conecuh County in central Alabama. They spent their early years with their parents where they worked in the fields from the time they were 6 years old.

    They were married in 1933, the worst year of the Great Depression, but things would commence to improve, slowly, from then on. The newly elected President, Franklin Delano Roosevelt, began to put in place government projects that provided work for nearly all the unemployed. The newly married couple was young and wanted to move to an area where they might have a better life. One of Sam's cousins lived near Mobile and worked at a sawmill. It was a large sawmill that owned its own timberland and had been in business for the past 30 years. Cousin Ira thought that Sam could get a job at the mill. There were shanties at the mill site furnished by the mill owner, where he and Susie could live rent free if he were an employee.

Sam and Susie moved to Creola and Sam did get a job at the mill. His first assignment was "doodling dust" from under the saw and the pay was 50 cents per day. Wages were paid every week, not in "coin of the realm" but in sawmill tokens that could only be spent in the company commissary or company store. However the commissary had all the goods needed, from groceries to clothing. Since the owner paid wages only in "sawmill checks" he could be sure that all the wages paid would be spent in the company-owned commissary.

It was common practice during those times for the mill owner to pay in sawmill tokens and to provide a commissary for the workers. This type of system allowed the mill owner to have complete control over his employees.

Susie Hairston was the best cook for miles around. She had learned to cook by helping her mother in the kitchen when she was young. The mill superintendent's wife was up in years and she needed help around the house, especially in the kitchen. It was by chance that Susie was able to begin work for her because their regular cook took down with the fever and later passed away. Susie was doing the housework at the time the cook got sick and the lady of the house asked her to help with the cooking. The first day she prepared chicken and dumplings. Everyone thought it was the best chicken they had ever eaten. From that day on, Susie was the cook at the "big house" and her pay was 50 cents per day in sawmill tokens. There was another benefit for her work in the kitchen because she was allowed to take some of the left-over food home for Sam's supper, which helped out considerably by saving money on the groceries. Now that Sam and

Susie were both working things were going well for the two of them in those early years of the Depression. Too soon things would change.

When President Roosevelt was elected he commenced to make radical changes in the way things were being done, or in some cases, not being done at all. One of the changes that were made affected the sawmill business very terribly. Roosevelt put into law the National Recovery Act (NRA) and one of the provisions in this act called for a minimum wage for all workers. The new law required the sawmill owner to pay a minimum of 25 cents per hour! This sort of thing had never been heard of in the southern states. Maybe the big manufacturing plants in the north could pay this sort of exorbitant wage. There was no way the owner of the sawmill would meet these wage requirements.

The owner closed down the sawmill and laid off all the workers. It was a tough blow for Sam but Susie was able to keep her job working as the cook, for the NRA did not control what they paid her as a domestic. Since she worked for the superintendent, she and Sam could still live in the company shanty rent free. They hoped Sam could find at least part time work in the area.

The mill stayed closed for 3 months but finally the owner gave in and met the NRA wage requirements. Sam went back to work at the mill and his new wage of 25 cents per hour was wonderful! The mill now operating under the new law did not operate full time, but the difference in pay made a much better life for the employees under the new rate. Part time pay under the new law provided more than they had ever made working full time in the past.

Sam remained at the mill until 1940, when the shipyards in Mobile commenced to hire workers. Cousin Ira had left the mill when it closed temporarily and he moved to Mobile. Workers were pouring into Mobile every day to fill the vacancies created for workers by the six shipyards now operating in the area. Sam and Susie moved into the boarding house with Cousin Ira's kin. The next day, Sam showed up at the gate to the shipyard with a group of 30 other people looking for work. That day all 30 were hired, including Sam.

135

Housing became scarce in Mobile, and some property owners were cleaning out their garages and renting them for sleeping quarters. Sam and Susie stayed on at the boarding house. Susie had a full time job in the kitchen of the boarding house and with Sam's pay at the shipyard they were making it "big time"! After Sam's first year in the shipyard, he qualified for the position of apprentice ship fitter, and after the year of apprenticeship, his pay was 2 dollars per hour. Sam was declared an essential worker, so he received a deferment from service when World War II was declared, and the military draft was instated. Many of the younger men who worked in the shipyard were drafted. By the end war, Sam had been promoted to the position of ship fitter and was drawing a good salary. He worked there until he retired. Sam and Susie saved their money and were able to purchase a small home in Creola, where they moved upon retirement.

Sam and Susie both had been brought up as members of the AME Church in Conecuh County. They became members of the AME church in Creola and Sam became a deacon of the church. Being retired gave him time for his favorite pursuit, fishing. Sam had a new Ford car which he purchased with some of his retirement pay, so he and Susie could visit their kinfolks in central Alabama. Being retired with a pension after all those years of hard work was wonderful and life was good for the two of them. They lived to a ripe old age and passed away within 3 months of each other. They were buried in the cemetery just off the Bluff Road near the river

Chapter Eight

The DiCarlo Family

Anthony and Maria DiCarlo immigrated to the United States in 1912. They had just gotten married and were seeking a new place to start their life together. Anthony came first in order to find a place to live and a job. He was sponsored by an old and dear friend, Marco Rossi who provided him a place to stay upon arrival in New York.

When he arrived at the Immigration Authority on Ellis Island in New York Harbor, his friend Marco was there to greet him and vouch for his sponsorship. After a week of processing, he left Ellis Island and joined Marco and his family in New York.

Anthony was a young, accomplished stonecutter and stone mason. His friend and sponsor, Marco found him a job as a stone mason with a building contractor in Boston. The first job he worked on was rebuilding the large, main post office that had burned in the great Boston fire, which had swept through the city a few years before. The job lasted for 2 years. He sent for his wife, Maria, now that he had a permanent position and a good salary coming in every week. He found a small one-bedroom apartment for the two of them and it was ready when his wife arrived at the Immigration Authority in Boston Harbor.

The project in Boston was completed, and since his work was good, he was able to get his next job in Portland, Maine, cutting stone for the new Regional Bank Building. As soon as he was settled on the new job, he sent for his wife in Boston. After 3 years on the job in Portland, he had saved enough money to buy a 5 acre lot at the edge of the city.

Now that he had land, he started building the family home. His property was located in an area where other Italian immigrants had settled and his neighbors would be there to help him build his new home. Construction would start as soon as he was able to purchase the materials needed. The property was located adjoining a large vegetable farm and a dairy. This would prove to be an excellent advantage as his family grew and as the Great Depression set in. Stone cutting and masonry work was in good demand up until the stock market failure in 1929. After this catastrophe, work was slow but Anthony became the maintenance man and groundskeeper for a very wealthy family who lived on a large estate on Cape Elizabeth. The estate contained a mansion on a 20 acre plot of seaside land, overlooking Casco Bay. It was one of the most beautiful spots on the Cape. Anthony worked regularly throughout the years of the Great Depression for the owner of the estate.

Sofia was the eldest daughter of the five DiCarlo children and when she graduated from high school in the early 1930s she worked part time at the farm adjoining their home. She picked cucumbers, pulled carrots and cut cabbage. It was not a very rewarding job but it did provide food for the family, because she was paid in vegetables.

Later she got a job as an apprentice sales person in one of the large department stores downtown in Portland. Before World War II, she married a young Canadian immigrant, Pierre Chatel, who was a shoemaker. He had recently come to Portland to work in the shoe industry, for which the city was famous. As the war years approached, and the demand for shoes increased, she joined her husband in the shoe factory. Even after the war ended, they continued to work at the shoe factory until they retired.

Sofia and Pierre raised 4 children, all of whom became successful members of the community. The oldest child, Lauren, worked in a department store, which was her first job. When the war broke out with Japan, Portland became a very busy port for all types of ships and there were sailors in town all the time on shore leave. Lauren met a young Navy Ensign whose ship was in the harbor. Each time his ship would come in to port, she and Andrew saw a great deal of each other until his ship sailed again. After the war was over, they were married and his first duty station was San Francisco, California. After 3 years in California, Andrew's next duty station was in Kodiak, Alaska. The assignment lasted for 4 years. Andrew managed to stay in the service for 20 years and he retired as a Lieutenant Commander. He and Lauren then moved to Tampa, Florida, where they enjoyed the beaches and the sunshine, for neither of them cared for the snow and ice of the winters in Maine.

The next Chatel child was a son, Alton. He finished high school, and became an apprentice draftsman for an architectural firm. He was good in mechanical drawing classes at high school, and the firm needed young men that were skilled in construction drawing techniques. Within a few years, he became the chief draftsman for the company. When his salary reached the point where he could afford a wife, he married his high school sweetheart.

The third child of Pierre and Sofia was a daughter, Verona. She married a young man with whom she had gone to high school and they soon had a baby boy, and later a girl. Before her baby girl was 2 years old, her husband Steven, who worked for a high rise construction company, met an untimely death. He was working on the 10th floor

139

level of a building, hanging steel, when a high wind came up suddenly, causing him to fall to the ground, killing him instantly.

Verona was a young widow, but her husband was insured because the company covered all of their employees. The money she received was sufficient for her to care for the children until they entered school. She was also entitled to her husband's Social Security benefits, which she planned to use to pay for her children's college educations. After both children graduated from the state university, she took a job as an office clerk.

The fourth Chatel child was Edward. He left Maine when he finished high school, to live in Boston, where went to work as a foremen in a manufacturing plant.

Martina was the second DiCarlo child. She spent some time picking produce on the farm next door to their home, like her older sister had. She got a job as a janitor for one of the downtown retail stores, after graduating from high school. During the early years of the war, she married a young sailor, named Edward Brent, and after the war they settled in Portland. Her husband worked for one of the metal fabricators until he retired. Their family consisted of three wonderful boys. The oldest boy entered the ministry. He became an evangelist and accepted a position as the pastor of a small evangelical church in west Texas, near the Rio Grande River.

Martina's second son, Abner Brent, became a nurse in the general hospital in Portland. While working there he met an older woman who was also a nurse and she was a widow. They worked together for several years, became good friends and eventually, decided to marry. Since she had worked at the hospital longer than Abner, she retired first and became a housewife to take care of the home while Abner continued to work for several more years. When the time came for him to retire, they moved out to Old Orchard Beach and bought a small cottage near the shore.

The third Brent son, Arturo, was the studious one of the family. He received a scholarship to the state university where he majored in electronics with a specialty in computers. He was hired after graduation by one of the large computer firms to service their rental units overseas.

Francesca DiCarlo graduated from high school two years before the war and had a job in a dress manufacturing plant in town. She was such a good seamstress that she was soon elevated to making the company salesmen's samples for them to take with them to show the company products.

When Pearl Harbor was attacked, she felt she should do her part in the war. She went down to the recruiting office and joined the Women's Army Corps. She completed basic training, and applied for Officers Training School. She was accepted and four months later she graduated with a commission in the Army as a Second Lieutenant. Her first duty station was at Edgewood Arsenal in Maryland, where she was assigned as the Special Service Officer for the post. She remained at this post until the war was over and then she was transferred to Boston, a post nearer home, where she met and married a young Captain in the Army. Francesca and her husband got out of the Army and used their G.I. Bill benefits to go to college, after which they moved to Florida.

When the war began in Korea, Francesca's husband was recalled to active duty from the Army Reserves and sent to Austria, with a Special Construction battalion. His unit's assignment was to supervise the construction of a 10,000-man Army camp near Salzburg. The camp was to become the headquarters for the military units on occupation duty. When housing in the private sector for military dependents became available, Francesca and their new baby were able to join him in Salzburg. He rented a new apartment on the east side of Salzburg with a wonderful view of the Austrian Alps. Her husband was Adjutant of the Special Construction Battalion.

They returned to the U.S. after his tour of duty was finished in Austria. They had one child who finished high school at the local Christian school. After high school, she attended the Christian college in Cleveland, where she majored in music. After graduation she obtained a teaching position in the local Christian high school.

Sara DiCarlo graduated from high school during the war years and married her high school sweetheart as soon as they graduated. She got a job with a canvas product company, sewing tents and awnings. Her husband was a draftsman for a local manufacturer. With both working, they were soon able to save enough to purchase a small cottage on Cape Elizabeth, where they lived and raised their family. They had three sons. The eldest son obtained a scholarship to the state university where he majored in education. His first year out of the university after graduation was spent teaching in the local high school. Each year during summer vacation from teaching, he returned to the university to study for his master's degree. When he received his master's degree, he was qualified for a teaching position at the local branch of the university. He retired from teaching after 20 years. He and his wife bought a condo at Fort Myers, Florida, where they spent their retirement years basking in the sun.

Sara's second son, Alfred, earned his degree from the university extension school. He paid his way by working in the sardine canneries located at the waterfront in Portland. Each summer vacation from school, and many nights and weekends, he continued to work at the cannery until he graduated. His degree was in business administration, so when he graduated the owner of the cannery hired him for a job in the office. Alfred's first assignment was to streamline the business's management, making it more efficient so that daily production, daily sales, daily profits could be easily determined.

The third son, William, had no desire to attend college. Instead, he wanted to be golf professional. He got a job right out of school at the local country club. There at the club, he could learn the game from the pros and he could do all the practice that his time off the job would allow. It was a natural for the young man, and after several years on the job, he was promoted to greens-keeper. Eventually, he gave up golf after he failed to achieve professional player status. His next job was as a manager of a fast food restaurant. It was hard work and long hours but the pay was good and he saved his money. Before long William had enough money in the bank that he could commence to invest in some venture. His father told him of some rundown houses that could be purchased for a small down payment. He was told that some of the houses just needed a few minor repairs, then could be rented out for more than enough to make his monthly payments. It was an opportunity that William could handle and was the start of his business enterprise. Before the year was out he acquired two rental houses and he had money coming in from them each month.

During the next few years William acquired a number of houses, and rental units, and they paid off well. He now had a full time job keeping his houses in good condition and fully rented. It took 10 years to pay off the first four houses. Using the cash coming in from his rental houses every month, he purchased a 10-unit apartment building, and began to really make big money. Owning the apartment building allowed him to sit back and manage his business enterprises. No, he never married. When asked, he said that he just could not spare the time from his business to manage a family.

Lorenzo DiCarlo was the only boy in the family. He was drafted just as soon as the war began with Japan. He served in the Pacific with the 71st Infantry Division. Their first operation was the recapture of Guam from the Japanese. The amphibious assault landings on the beaches of Guam were a real disaster. The Navy Operations command had made a mistake as to what hour the tides on the beaches would be full on the south side of Guam. It was imperative that the amphibious assault be at the very highest tide of the day, for the coastal area of Guam, where the landing was to take place, was completely protected by coral reefs extending out a half mile from the beach. At low tide the landing craft could not get any closer than several hundred yards of the beach. The assault landing was scheduled for daybreak, which, as it happened, was the time of the lowest tide of the day in the landing area but the assault boats proceeded toward the beach regardless of the tide conditions.

The Japanese had anticipated that if the island was attacked by the Allied Forces, it would be on the beach where the landing actually was taking place. Machine gun positions were set up to cover the entire area where the reefs existed. Heavy artillery was deployed in the dense jungle 300 yards back from the beach and they were zeroed in on the area of the reefs. The enemy had set the trap and the amphibious assault troops would be cut to ribbons as their landing craft hung up on the reefs where they were sitting ducks for the guns on shore. The first landing craft trapped on the reefs were demolished by the artillery on shore. Next were the machine gun and mortar squads that were assigned to set up an outer perimeter of defense on the beach. These troops were in alligators, a tracked tank-like vehicle that was both a boat and a land vehicle. When the alligators got to the reefs they could crawl over the coral and continue over the remaining reefs to the beach.

Machine guns were mounted on the alligators which allowed the crew to rake the beach with heavy fire as they approached the landing, so that they could knock out the Japanese machine guns that were firing on the boats behind them on the reefs. Then the troops could move into the beach and concentrate their fire power in the area of the enemy artillery positions. The first machine gun crews secured the beach landing area and the alligators went back to the landing party and brought in more troops over the reefs. The first two days at Guam were a disaster for the 71st Division. Dozens of troops were lost on the reefs from Japanese gunfire and many more were wounded. By the second day all the troops were ashore and moved out to silence the enemy artillery. As the enemy moved into the jungles, the division troops followed until most of the enemy were killed or captured with the remainder of them lost in the jungles. Lorenzo's unit moved to the Philippine Islands after Guam had been secured where the division participated in reclaiming the northern peninsular of Luzon. When the war ended his division was designated to become occupation troops in Japan. Lorenzo's regiment shipped out of the Philippines on 7 October 1945, bound for the port of Otaru, on the island of Hokkaido. Their duty was to supervise and assist the Japanese in developing a stable government and to see that the peace was kept. In November 1945, the unit was relieved of duty.

Chapter Nine

Arthur

The story of the young man on page 173

More of the problems of the Depression years are described in the following story of a young man who lived through those times. Arthur was born shortly after the close of World War I. He was the first son and second child of a family of very modest means. It could be said that he came into this world at an interesting time. It was the year that women were permitted to vote, airplanes were commencing to be seen frequently in the skies and the all-knowing fathers in Washington had passed legislation outlawing the sale and manufacturer of liquor in any form. His father had been employed by the railroad until 1922, when the economy began to falter and slow down after the close of the war. For the next four years the family operated a small subsistence farm on rented land in south Alabama. The young lad started school at the age of five in a rural two room school, which he attended for five years. After his fifth year, the county schools were consolidated. The small two room schools were closed and the children were bused fifteen miles away from home to a large urban elementary school. The consolidation improved the quality of education for these rural students, who could then benefit from interaction with a larger student body and from the teaching of better qualified instructors.

By the time Arthur was six years old he was helping with chores around the house. One of his first responsibilities was the filling of the wood boxes at the cook stove and the large fireplace every evening when he came in from school. His next evening chore was to pump water at the well for the cattle as they came in from the pasture to be milked.

Arthur was still in the fourth and fifth grades in elementary school, when he began fur trapping. His Uncle Herbert was an

145

accomplished hunter who provided meat for the table and furs for sale. Arthur wanted to earn some spending money, so he learned to trap fur animals from his uncle. There were plenty of fur bearing animals around in the woods adjoining the farm and the creek bottoms nearby. All one had to do was learn to catch these animals and how to care for the skins and prepare them for the market. On the weekends, Arthur and his dog, Old Tobey, would search the area around the farm for signs where foxes had been traveling at night, or where striped polecats had been holed up, or where beavers had built their underwater dens. They would look for signs where raccoons, looking for frogs and small fish had made trails along the creek banks. Those locations were all good places to set traps. The traps were set out in the evening and they had to be checked for catches early in the morning. If the traps were successful in making a catch the animal had to be taken from the trap and the skin removed carefully, all the fat cleaned from the skin and the pelt was stretched on a drying frame right away.

There was a good market all through the Depression years for animal pelts. A good red fox pelt or a large raccoon pelt sold for $1.75, a striped polecat skin fetched 65 cents, and a beaver was a real catch for they sold for $3.00. Possums, the most plentiful animal in the area, sold for 50 cents.

Arthur was shipping several pelts per month to the fur buyers in St. Louis, Missouri. Some months he would make up to $15.00. The money was a real fortune for a young man at that time. He was able to buy a pair of knee high lace-up boots, a pair of knee length whipcord breeches, a heavy wool shirt and a small 22 caliber rifle. At that time, the rifle was an expensive, luxury item as it cost $5.50, but it was a necessary item for a hunter-trapper. The fur trapping had to stop when he entered high school for he did not have time to set the traps, run the trap lines, and complete his school work, too.

Arthur enrolled in the large urban high school just as most of the banks failed in 1932. To attend high school he had to have transportation daily for a trip of twenty miles each way. His elder sister drove the family car the first year and after she graduated, he got a job with a neighbor who owned a small dairy. The dairy needed someone to deliver milk daily to their customers in Mobile. The job required that he be at the dairy by four o'clock in the morning. The dairy owner's wife would have breakfast ready when the young man arrived. After breakfast, he would load the milk in the Willys Overland truck and deliver it door to door in Mobile. The delivery of the milk was complete before classes started at school.

After school was over for the day, he returned the empty milk bottles he had picked up to the dairy. When he got home he had chores to do. The first thing was to change into work clothes and feed the hogs, then the chickens, and then bring the cows in from the pasture. His mother would milk the cows in the morning during school days but he did the milking in the evenings and on weekends. After the milking was done and the animals were fed, the wood boxes had to be filled. Supper was usually early in the evening and after that there was homework to be done by lamplight. It made a busy day for young Arthur but in those Depression days it was the way of life for many.

The summer after his first year of high school, Arthur worked at a filling station for 50 cents a day. There he pumped gasoline for the customers, washed their windshields, checked the oil level in the engine, checked water level in the radiator and checked the tire pressure. In those days a full service station had to provide these services with a gasoline purchase. During the summer after the second year of school, he got a better summer job working in a garage. He was paid $5.00 a week for a six-day work week. It was a good job for the times. He was able to keep the job at the garage each summer until he graduated from high school.

The summer Arthur finished his third year in high school he bought a car. It was a 1923 Model T Ford touring car. The top was missing but the tires were good and the motor would run. He found the car stowed away in a barn and the owner said it had been in the barn for several years. He asked the man who owned it how much he would take for the car. His price was $15.00 but Arthur only had $10.00. The farmer decided since the car had been in the barn for a long time and he had no use for it anyway, he would go ahead and sell it for $10.00. Arthur spent the next few days checking out his new purchase, filled it with motor oil, filled the radiator, and filled the gas tank. After a few priming cranks the engine fired off and started. Arthur had wheels! He kept the Ford for over a year, then sold it to another kid for $15.00.

Upon finishing high school, he took on his old job at the garage full time. He began work at seven in the morning and worked all day six days each week for $5.50 a week. The work consisted of changing engine oil, greasing cars, and cleaning engine parts, adjusting carburetors, changing tires and helping with engine overhauls. Soon he had money enough to pursue his dream of becoming an airplane pilot. One of his uncles was a Navy aviator whom he greatly admired, and he wanted very much to become a pilot, himself. Arthur's father didn't think that flying was a smart thing to do for such an endeavor was not safe. Didn't he remember that his uncle had crash landed two times? He spoke with his mother about flying and she told him that if there had been airplanes when she was young, she surely would have become a pilot. That was enough to convince Arthur to take lessons at the local airport.

In those days flight training in a Piper Cub or a Gypsy Moth cost $1.75 per half hour of instruction. If the student learned fast he could receive his Student Permit after one acceptable solo flight and eight hours of flying time. A Private Pilot License could be obtained after 30 hours of satisfactory flying time. Arthur enjoyed flying and each week he would take an hour of instruction and flying time and even more if he could afford the cost. Within a few weeks he had qualified for his Student Permit, and could go on to a Private Pilot License as he earned the money to pay for the lessons.

He took a placement test to try for a position with the State Highway Department as an engineering aide. His qualifying score placed him near the top of the list to be hired when a vacancy became available. It was nearly two years before a vacancy opened with the State. It was a desirable position, which paid $42.00 per month. A job of that nature was a dream for a young man even if the work required long hours for the entire week. It was more money than he had ever thought he could he possibly earn. He was an engineering aide working with the project surveyor and the project engineer on new highway construction projects.

The job was in a rural county in west central Alabama. He lived in a boarding house with three other young men who worked for the state. The price of room and board, $5.00 a month, included a nice, clean bed, three meals a day, laundry once a week. He now had $37.00 free and clear each month, and money to start a bank account for the first time in his life. Every payday, he deposited his check in the bank.

It was in this small town that Arthur found his first real girlfriend. Up to this time, he had been so busy trying to make a few dollars that he had no time for the beautiful young ladies and besides he didn't really know any of them back home. Now that he had a good regular job, money in the bank and free time on the weekends and sometimes in the evenings he felt that he deserved to have a girlfriend. All the other guys had one.

Geanie and Arthur met at the local drug store one Saturday evening. The young soda jerk behind the counter introduced them telling her that Arthur was the new guy who had just come to work with the state. He told Geanie that he lived at his mother's boarding house over by the cemetery. Arthur found out the next day that Geanie had just graduated from high school the week before he reported for duty. The soda jerk filled him in with all the details: she had a new Ford V-8 sedan that her father gave her for a graduation gift, her family owned the large farm where they lived, just outside of town, and they were one of the founding families of the area.

Geanie was a doll. Red hair, freckled face and she stood five foot six in her stocking feet. From the very first day that Arthur met her, he knew he wanted her for his very own. Time, circumstance, and international affairs were all determined to deny Arthur of his first love. Every young single man in town would have given his last pair of new shoes to ride in that Ford sedan but there was one small problem. Mama said that little brother, Geanie's ten year old brother, had to go along with her any time she had a boy in the car. The mandate by Geanie's mama bothered the other would-be suitors but Arthur didn't mind. Her brother was a good kid who minded his manners and did not interfere when the three of them were on an outing in the car.

Arthur's job with the state was as a soil inspector where the big machines were moving earth to form a new road bed. One day after Arthur had met Geanie, he was working near town when she and her little brother drove out to watch the construction. At least that was the excuse she used. She said her little brother was fascinated by the big Caterpillars that were moving the earth on the roadway. Arthur asked him if he would like to ride on one of the big machines and he said yes. One of the graders was flagged down and Arthur boosted the boy up into the cab and asked the operator to take him for a ride. The operator rode the young fellow around for an hour or so.

The interlude gave the Geanie and Arthur plenty of time to become acquainted. You might say they got to know each other during this time. Arthur felt that she must be attracted to older men, like him, for he was almost 21. She and her brother came every day for the remainder of the week and each time Arthur would get the boy a ride on one of the "Big Cats". Each day the doll and Arthur found that they had a great deal in common, primarily a great desire to see more of each other.

When she came to visit to the job site on Friday, Arthur asked to take her to the movies on Saturday night. She agreed, but said he would have to come home with her and ask Mama. He went. After a stern lecture concerning how to behave, what not to do, and when to come home, he was approved on a trial basis. From then on it was a regular thing for the three of them, Arthur, Geanie, and the little brother, to go to the movies on Saturday night.

On weekends and evenings after work, she would meet Arthur at the drug store, where they would share an ice cream soda. It was one of those slightly romantic things where they had one soda and two straws and if it was done correctly both could sip from the glass at the same time. That brought the two pretty close to kissing distance but that never happened in public. They only wanted those envious boys that hung around the drug store to think they might. Arthur felt like a king walking around town with the prettiest girl on his arm and with all of the other boys looking on.

Geanie and Arthur were getting along well by late summer. She would come by and pick him up every Sunday after church and the three of them would go riding in the new Ford sedan. Yes, her brother was with them, Mama's order, you know. The arrangement was okay with Arthur for he was a good kid and always wanted to sit in the front seat by the window, which, of course, squeezed Geanie in the middle between him and Arthur.

The brother was pretty smart. He knew they would appreciate some time without him being underfoot. He usually got lost when they stopped at the old abandoned Meeting House or a favorite spot along the sandy creek bank so they could smooch a little. Of course they were discreet for they didn't want the little one to carry any tales of indiscretion back to Mama. As far as they knew, he never did. Arthur felt his position with Geanie was secure for none of the other boys wanted to go out with a girl who had to take along a kid brother, even if she did have a new Ford sedan.

They spent as much time together as they could all summer. Every Saturday night they went to the movies, meetings at the drug store for a soda and trips to Bradford's Pond for a boat ride listening to the sweet refrains that were playing on the juke box. "Maria Elena" was one of the most popular songs that year. Arthur gave her the ring and a gold watch and pledged his love to her forever. But on 7 December 1941, all hell broke loose and the country was plunged into a four year war with Japan. That changed everything for Geanie and Arthur.

He had just turned 21 the month before Pearl Harbor was bombed and he was sure to be drafted for military service. He decided to go ahead and enlist before he was drafted. The following week he gave the state notice that he intended to join the military service. When he went to enlist, he requested to join the Army Air Corps and become an Air Cadet. When he took the physical examination to

151

qualify for flight training it was discovered he did not have perfect eye sight. This fact was enough to disqualify him for flight training. The Personnel Office suggested since he was a qualified pilot in small planes he could become a liaison pilot of a spotter plane for an artillery battalion. He enlisted in the 195th Heavy Artillery Battalion and saw action in New Guinea and in the Philippine Islands as a recon pilot for three years until the war was over.

At Arthur's going-away party, Geanie and the boys who worked with him wished him well. Geanie made him promise to take good care of himself and come home safely. Arthur's replacement on the state job was young man by the name of Thomas and he was there that evening at the party. He was a tall, good looking young man of the age to enter service but he would wait and let them draft him. At Arthur's party, Thomas met Geanie for the first time. they seemed to hit it off but Arthur felt his position with Geanie was secure and something special. Thomas would be drafted soon and he would pose no threat to Arthur's relationship with Geanie.

Arthur and Geanie promised to write to each other faithfully and they did. Before Arthur's military unit left Florida for the west coast, where they would prepare to leave for overseas duty, Geanie came down to camp for a short visit. They talked about their engagement and their plans to be married as soon as the war was over. They both prayed the war would be a short one so they could go on with their lives as planned. Before going overseas, Arthur was given a ten-day leave to go home. Most of that ten days Arthur spent with Geanie and the fire of love was still there. It seemed now to be stronger than ever. The time came so quickly for Arthur to report back to camp from leave. There was a long embrace, loving kiss, and a tearful departure. Now they must wait. The first six weeks overseas were very busy for Arthur and there were times when it was impossible to write. Letters from Geanie arrived once a week for the first six months and then they began to space out. Arthur did not know until later that Thomas had been drafted about the time his unit left Florida. He was sent overseas as a member of an armored tank crew, was wounded in North Africa on his first assignment, and sent home to recuperate. Thomas's home was in Sulphur Springs and Geanie's home was in Bladen-only three miles away.

Soon Geanie's letters were only coming monthly, or every six weeks or more, and she was not saying how much she missed Arthur. She was telling how poor Thomas was shot up so bad. She told Arthur how she visited him now and then to check on him and his healing process. Then Geanie's letter even less frequent, with more information about poor Thomas and the closing of the letters was "Take care of yourself over there in the jungles" instead of "I love you so much, I can hardly wait for the war to end." It commenced to dawn on Arthur that something had changed drastically back in paradise with his fiancée. Geanie no longer seemed to be completely and devotedly Arthur's intended future bride. Her letters led him to believe she was being distracted by some local, outside influence. He could hardly believe it, because they had pledged their love to each other until the war was over and the war was damn sure not over yet.

Arthur graduated from Officers Training School and was commissioned a Second Lieutenant. He sent her a picture of him with his new rank and uniform and told her the good news. The following day at mail call he received a letter from Geanie. She wrote "I am sorry to be the one to have to tell you this, but if I don't, your mother will, very soon, for the by the time you receive this letter, Thomas and I will have been married. He needs someone to watch over him while he is healing and regaining his strength. I could not bear to see him suffer alone. I have sent your ring back to your mother. Take care of yourself, Geanie."If Arthur had not been so busy with the war and everything, the turn of events would probably have bothered him a great deal. You may want to ask If Arthur went to see Thomas and Geanie after the war was over and he returned home. Sure, he did. It was good to see them both and their two little tykes. Arthur knew they had their hands full but what about Thomas? Oh, he healed up just fine, in fact, you couldn't tell he had ever been in the war. In fact, Arthur thought to himself, Thomas's war was just about to start.

153

Author's Note: Dear John and Dear Jane letters such as described in this story about Arthur and Geanie occurred very frequently during the war years. A young lady finds love in the arms of a 4-fer while her intended love has his time occupied at the war front. She breaks the news by writing "Dear John" I married your best friend. Of course, she spoils John's day and then some. Most Dear John letter recipients took the disappointment very seriously. One such Navy seaman "Dear John" jumped overboard from his ship while at sea after receiving his letter. He was never seen again. "Dear Janes" were sometimes the case when a serviceman, having met a beautiful young lady at a USO dance, fallen in love at first sight, and presented her with a ring to become engaged, would then, on his trip home on leave, meet his old girlfriend. Soon he writes "Dear Jane" I guess we were not meant for each other, for while I was home on leave, I found that I am still in love with Margaret."

Arthur had been promoted to Chief Warrant Officer, by the end of the war, and he chose to get out of the Service and go to college. He entered the state university, eventually graduating with a degree in Civil Engineering. He went back to work for the Alabama State Highway Department, where he worked before the war. It became his life's work and he remained with the state until he retired at age 60.

At the end of the war there were thousands of surplus war planes, which the government stored in the desert, in Arizona. There were acres of planes of all types parked there in row after row. They were offered for sale and most could be bought at the price you were willing to offer. Arthur had flown the L-4 and L-5 Piper liaison planes, and he wished to have his own plane. He went to Arizona to check out the Pipers that were available. He purchased an L-5 Piper for $500.00. It was a real find and since he had always dreamed of having his own personal plane, now the dream had come true. He happily flew it back to Montgomery.

Chapter Ten

The Model T Ford & Life in the 1920s

1927 Model T Ford

    In 1923, a Model T Ford Touring car cost $300.00 cash money. There was no such thing as time payments in order to purchase an automobile. That form of usury did not come into vogue until much later. You paid for the car before you drove it home.

The touring car had a canvas top, side curtains to keep out the rain and some of the cold wind and celluloid windows. It was a three door model. There was not a door on the driver's side of the car.

A simple driving lesson was provided with the car sale. This was necessary because most first-time car buyers had no idea how to even start the car, or operate it. The salesman would usually give the new owner a lesson on driving their new vehicle. The lesson consisted of a trip around the block and up the street a ways. All the time the salesman would be telling how to start, stop and use the gear pedals. The new owner then would handle the driving on the way back to the car lot.

When the deal was completed, the new vehicle would have a full tank of gasoline, the engine would be filled with oil, and the radiator would be checked for the proper amount of water. How different from today where you pay $25,000.00for a new car and they only put enough gas in the tank to get you off the car lot.

Model Ts were a cantankerous lot, for they were difficult to start and they had to be hand cranked. There were no electric starters, and in fact, there were no batteries either. They steered like an oxcart and it was rough riding on the hard seats. The seats were filled with horse hair and covered with heavily lacquered leather. There was always a strong smell of burned oil, grease, gasoline and exhaust fumes. They were cold in the winter for they had no heater. Ignition was provided by a magneto and a set of four coils. These coils were sometimes a real problem during rainy weather, because if they got wet, the car stopped. The car would not start again until the coils had been removed from the engine compartment and thoroughly dried. Drying was a problem for the coils were embedded in tar and placed in a wooden box. If the coils were heated too hot in order to dry them, all the tar would run out and the coils would be ruined. The coils were normally taken out of the car during rainy weather and into the house where they would stay warm and dry.

You had to be careful that the spark lever was set just right when cranking the engine. If the spark lever was set too high, the engine might kick back causing the cranking lever to break the cranker's arm. This sort of accident happened quite frequently. In the old days, no one thought of putting the car in a garage. Houses were not built with garages back then. If the car needed to be put under a shelter, then one of the stalls in the barn would be cleaned out and the car driven into the barn.

Most first-time automobile owners during the early years ,also had a horse and buggy or a surrey for transportation. When they bought their first car they were not sure how reliable it would be, so they kept their horses and buggies, just in case.

Despite all its faults, the Model T Ford was something everyone wanted in the early 1920s.

Auto Travel in the 1920s

After the Wilson family moved from central Alabama to the Gulf Coast area near Mobile in the mid-twenties, each year they would make a trip back to central Alabama to see their folks. The trips were made in a Model T Ford sedan around August, each year before school started. A typical journey took about two days one way and the distance was nearly 200 miles. There was only three blocks of brick paving and one traffic signal on the whole trip. Most of the roads were gravel, just plain dirt, or mud. There was one large river to cross by ferry. One must remember that the Model T Ford was not a fast automobile. Its top speed on good roads was 30 mph, but seldom was the road suitable for such high speed. The average speed was 20-25 mph on good roads.

Crossing the river on the ferry was most times a problem. It was time consuming and often almost impossible to get across the river in half a day. The small barge ferry could only take one car over and bring one car back on each two hour crossing. The big problem arose when the river was at flood stage and out of its banks. The ferry could not operate when the river was flooding, due to the swift currents and floating debris. If the traveler happened to arrive at the ferry site at flood stage, he either went back the way he came or camped out three or four days until the water receded. On most trips it took the family only a half day to get across the river. There was swamp and mud on the west side, and on the east side there was a steep red clay hill that was almost impossible to negotiate after a heavy rainfall. Normally, on a good day, the family would get across the river by noon, and proceed on north to Jackson and Grove Hill. A few miles north of Grove Hill, there was a real nice camping site off the road at a good spring of water and a large oak tree to camp under. Usually they would camp there for the night, unless some other travelers had arrived and claimed the site first.

In preparing for the trip, the family would load a tent, cooking pots and an iron skillet into the car. Enough food would be packed such as smoked ham, sausage, eggs, lard, etc. for a few days on the road. The tent would be set up upon arrival at the camp site, water would be brought from the spring, dry wood would be gathered for the fire and supper would be prepared. After a good night's sleep under the stars, they would rise early, fix breakfast, cleanup, pack up and be ready to go about daylight, for another day on the road. Depending on the number of flat tires and other mishaps they would encounter, they would arrive at their grandmother's house about sundown on the second day.

Usually they stayed at their grandmother's house for nearly a week. At that time of year, everything on the large farm was almost ready to be harvested. There was a large fruit orchard with plenty of apples, pears, peaches and plums, and there was always dried fruit to take home. If the visit happened to be at syrup-making time, it an adventure for the children to watch as the cane was being squeezed to get out the juice and then watch the juice being boiled in the pan to make it into syrup.

The trip home for the Wilsons was another two day affair, with good luck. There was always the chance that the river might be at flood stage and there was always the chance of car trouble. In the 1920s, autos were not very dependable. If the engine lasted 10,000 miles without a major breakdown, you were lucky. Bearings could wear out long before they should. Pistons would sometimes burst and valves would burn out. Any of these problems were a major repair job. If such a problem should occur in the countryside, it was most difficult to find a mechanic that could repair the vehicle, even if he could get the parts.

Prices during the Troublesome Years

The prices of everyday items during the 1930s were unbelievable in comparison to the prices of the same items after the turn of the current century. Gasoline was regularly priced at 16 to 18 cents per gallon. Some service stations would put on special sales that were referred to at that time as gas wars, and the price per gallon would be reduced to 12 cents. Daily newspapers were 5 cents and the Sunday paper was 25 cents.

Candy bars were real bargains in the old days. The chocolate bar was 5 cents and it was larger than the same bar that sells today for over a dollar. Coca-Cola was 5 cents a bottle and it was the same bottle that sells today for a dollar or more. A box of soda crackers was a nickel. Cheese was 25 cents a pound, bacon was the same price and coffee was 30 cents per pound. Eggs were 20 cents a dozen.

One dollar would buy a pair of men's shoes, pants were $1.25, men's suits started at $7.50, and dress shirts were 75 cents. There were "Five and Dime Stores" that actually had most of the items priced at 5 and 10 cents. At the soda fountain in those stores, a sandwich cost 10 cents. Ice creams, a cup of coffee or hot dogs were 5 cents each.

Many 40 acre farms, cleared and fenced with a nice 3-bedroom house, barn and outbuildings sold for $1500 to $1800. Rural undeveloped land sold for 25 cents to $1.25 per acre. Country homes did not have the luxury of electricity until the late 1940s. When the government funded the Rural Electric Administration, after the war, they built distribution lines to the rural areas. Homes outside the cities had no public water service. they had wells or hand-operated pumps. Public water systems for the rural homes did not become available until later in the 1950s. Many of the public roads and state highways were not paved in the 1930s.

A new modest wood frame home on a city lot sold for $3000 to $5000, and interest on the mortgage was from three fourth to one per cent. More expensive brick homes ranged in price from $8000 to $10,000.

New cars, in the 1920s, started at $375.00. The 1930s automobiles ranged in price from $500.00 to $800 each. The Packards and Pierce Arrows fell in the higher price range.

These prices seem ridiculous but they have to be considered with the conditions of the times in which they existed. During the troublesome years, day laborers earned 50 to 75 cents per day and skilled workers made twice the day laborer's pay. Clerks, waitresses and domestic help would be fortunate to make as much as a day laborer. In the Depression years, it was more difficult for a worker to have the 5 cents for the chocolate bar than it is for a present day worker to purchase the same chocolate bar for $1.25.

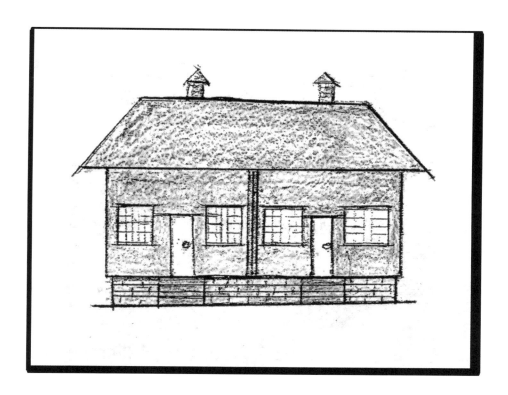

Two-Room Elementary Schools

The country elementary schools usually were located in each rural community. In the 1920s, there were no buses to haul children to the consolidated schools. This practice did not commence until the early 1930s. Some of the rural schools would have only a dozen or so children in each school.

One teacher would hold classes for the first four grades in one room and another teacher would teach the other grades in the other room. Each student had to provide their own books, writing paper, pencils, pens, ink and all other materials needed in class. There were no free school books in those days.

There was no cafeteria where food was served to the students or where they could buy their lunch. Each student had to bring their own lunch. Cafeterias were not a part of the schools until around 1935, when the bus system began and the schools were consolidated. Even then, the food in the cafeterias was not free. The students had to purchase what they ate or bring their own lunch from home.

In two-room schools, there were no indoor bathroom facilities. There were attached outhouses, one for the girls and one for the boys. They were four-holer privies attached to the school building by a covered walkway-sometimes. At some schools, the privies were set far out from the building in the school yard. During rainy or inclement weather, unless the student had an umbrella, getting relief was a real problem.

There were two coat closets in each school room, located on each side of the entrance, one for the boys and one for the girls. There was no such thing as air conditioning in those two-room schools. There were several large windows on both the outside walls so air could go into the room from both directions. The large windows gave plenty of light for the students to read by. The only other light was provided by a few light drops from the ceiling.

Winters were most trying in these small schools, for they were heated by a pot-bellied, cast iron upright heater in the center of the room. The heaters were fired with wood most of the time but some schools had coal-fired heaters. During the winter months, the teacher or someone from the community, had to come to the school early, and fire up the heater in order to warm the rooms before the children arrived. The children who sat near the heater were over-heated and the ones near the windows were cold most of the time. It was not a very good situation for learning. The students were too hot in the fall and spring and too cold during the winter. Each classroom had a large blackboard on the wall behind the teacher's desk, along the top of which, the alphabet was written in large script letters.

EPILOGUE

The Beginning of the War Years

The year 1941 was a year of apprehension and concern for everyone in the United States as well as the remainder of the world, due to the turmoil that Hitler and the Axis Powers were causing in Europe. Another worry was the long standing aggressive attitude of Japan in the Far East. Already Japan had shown an interest in taking over the American, British, Dutch and Australian interests in the Southwest Pacific and the East Indies areas. No one knew how far the Japanese war effort would extend nor was it known if they would become an active and effective partner of Hitler's Axis Powers. Beginning in the mid-thirties, Japan had embarked on an aggressive war with China after having subjected Manchuria to Japanese control. It was probable that Japan planned to take over most of Indonesia.

Japan was obviously gearing up for an extended operation of some sort. Many shiploads of scrap metal were brought into Japan from all over the world during the mid to late thirties. Manufactured goods were being stockpiled, especially those mechanical items that had to do with machinery and equipment. They were also storing crude petroleum products in quantities far in excess of their normal requirements.

In the United States the President had called up draftees for a two-year period of training. The draftees were trained as a military reserve to build up the armed forces in case of war. No one wanted the American troops committed to a war in Europe, the feeling was, let Europe fight its own war. We will help with supplies, ships and arms but not with troops. President Roosevelt stated, "Our boys will never serve overseas" but he had sympathy for England and her fight against a possible invasion from the Axis Powers. He knew the people of the United States would not support a declaration of war unless their own country was attacked. Most of the first draftees were scheduled to be

163

discharged in December, 1941. They never got the chance to be discharged because of the Japanese attack on Pearl Harbor on 7 December 1941. After war was declared against Japan, the early draftees had their tour of duty extended. The men became filler replacements for the regular army units in order to bring them up to combat strength and consequently were some of the first soldiers to enter combat in World War II.

With the declaration of war many things changed in the United States. Rationing of nearly everything began in order to conserve vital materials and products for the war effort. Shipyards worked around the clock to produce Naval fighting ships and Liberty ships for the transport of goods and troops. Automobile factories retooled and made aircraft. Factories commenced to operate at full capacity turning out war materiel and new military training camps were being built in every part of the country. At the peak of shipyard production, some companies were completing one Liberty ship each day in order to keep up with the losses of merchant marine ships to submarine warfare. The United States was providing ships for all of the Allied shipping needs, in addition to the replacement of Naval vessels that were destroyed at Pearl Harbor. There was a steady schedule of ships in convoys carrying materials through the North Atlantic to Murmansk in northern Russia. In addition to the draft, young men and women were volunteering for military service in record numbers.

Diplomatic relations between the United States and Japan fell apart during 1941 and one crisis followed another. By mid-November, war appeared inevitable and Saburo Kurusu, special Japanese "peace envoy" to the United States, arrived in San Francisco, en-route to Washington D.C., ostensibly to patch up the deep-rooted differences between the two countries. "I hope to break through the line and make a touchdown" Kurusu told reporters when he arrived in Washington. On December 7, 1941, Kurusu and Japanese Ambassador Admiral Kichisaburo Nomura called on Secretary of State, Cordell Hull, to discuss an exchange of diplomatic notes between the two countries. The visit started at 2:20 pm Sunday and before it was over Japanese bombs had fallen on Pearl Harbor, crippling the Pacific fleet and thrusting America into war. The next day, December 8, west of the International Date Line, Japanese bombs were dropped on the Philippine Islands, Guam, Wake Island, Singapore, and Hong Kong. In addition, on that date, Japanese forces invaded Thailand, and Malaya.

President Roosevelt had been vacationing at Warm Springs, Georgia. He had hurried back to Washington on December 2, upon receiving an urgent telephone call from Secretary Hull. Just before the Japanese attack, President Roosevelt sent a personal message to Japanese Emperor Hirohito asking that war be averted.

The blow at Pearl Harbor was a heavy one. Ten warships were put out of action and five of them were battleships. Casualties were 2,343 Army and Navy personnel killed, 1,272 wounded and 962 missing. Most of the Army and Navy planes there in Pearl Harbor and in the Philippine Islands were destroyed. On December 9, Japanese troops landed on the north and west coasts of Luzon Island, in the Philippines, after widespread air attacks. The same day the Japanese bombed Singapore and they tried to enter Hong Kong but were driven back. Thailand ceased resistance immediately and the international settlement at Shanghai, China, fell to the Japanese.

The Japanese moved fast in the early days of the war and on December 10, 1941 the British suffered one of their greatest naval losses. Japanese torpedo planes sank the British 35,000 ton Prince of Wales and the 32,000 ton Repulse. They were steaming north in order to ease the threat on Singapore by breaking up an assault landing by the Japanese on the Malay Peninsula. Admiral Husband E. Kimmel, Navy Commander of Pearl Harbor when the enemy blow fell, was replaced by Admiral Chester Nimitz, who was named head of the Navy. The Army commander at the time of the attack was Lieutenant General Walter C. Short. He was named head of the Army.

Meanwhile the Japanese opened a general offensive against Hong Kong, landed troops on Davao and threw thousands of reinforcements into Luzon Island. Japanese action was concentrated in Indo-China for an invasion of Burma. On December 17, 1941, Japanese troops landed on Borneo at the oil centers of Miri and Liang.

165

Control of the petroleum production in Borneo was most important for Japan in order to provide fuel for their war efforts.

The Japanese Domei News Agency disclosed that as early as January 24, 1942, Admiral Tsoroku Yamamoto, commander of the combined Japanese fleet had written: "I am looking forward to dictating peace demands to the United States in the White House in Washington." At a later date, the Admiral had also warned the warlords of Japan that they must strike fast and destroy the United States' capability to recover. If they did not, then the United States had the capacity to overcome and they would surely win any war against them. Yamamoto had lived, worked, and gone to school in the United States and he knew the ability of its industrial might

On December 4, 1941, Wake Island was reported lost after 389 defending Marines and seven Navy Medical Corpsmen held out for fourteen days against superior enemy forces. They were over whelmed after sinking seven Japanese warships, including a Japanese cruiser.

The Japanese bombed Manila causing heavy loss of life among civilians. They bombed Corregidor Fortress and demanded that the Americans surrender. At that time, Admiral Nimitz had taken over the crippled Pacific Fleet.

Hong Kong surrendered on Christmas Eve 1941. Singapore was placed under martial law and the Japanese shelled the Celebes and seized the Gilbert Islands. On January 31, 1942, Sir Archibald P. Wavell was named Supreme Commander in the Southwest Pacific and he set up headquarters at Java. Admiral Thomas C. Hart was commander of the almost non-existent Allied Fleet. The Japanese by this time were burning towns and shooting civilians in the Philippines.

On January 3, 1942 the Japanese bombed Rabaul, New Britain. By mid-January, the enemy tide of conquest had swept up eight of the nine Malay States. The Japanese bombed Tarakan Island, an oil rich island off the northeast coast of Borneo. They captured the island almost immediately on the same date the enemy soldiers invaded Burma and other troops were within 90 miles of Singapore.

General Douglas MacArthur was on Luzon Island in the Philippines carrying out his skillful defense of the island against an over whelming superiority. By January 21, 1942, his forces retreated to Bataan. The United States sent 600,000 troops and many planes to the Pacific but could not send any of them to the Philippines. Australian Imperials were fighting a bitter battle on New Britain. Lae, the capital of Australian New Guinea, had been evacuated before the Japanese troops arrived. Early in the war Australia appealed to the United States for aid in preventing a Japanese invasion of northern Australia.

The situation in the Southwest Pacific became darker as the Japanese overran the Celebes and all of Borneo. They swept towards Singapore and then demanded that General MacArthur surrender. On January 31, 1942, the British forces withdrew to Singapore Island after losing a fifty-four-day jungle battle to save the Malay States. Waves of Japanese bombers were blasting Singapore, Surabaya and Java every day. Japanese parachute troops were dropped on Sumatra.

Every victory had been Japan's until February 1, 1942. Admiral Nimitz then announced that a task force under Admiral William F Halsey had hit six Japanese naval and air bases in the Marshall and Gilbert Islands. Sixteen Japanese ships were sunk. Dutch Forces suffered severe losses in the bombardment of Surabaya. Thousands of miles away from Japan there were fierce air battles over Rangoon with General Claire Chennault's Flying Tigers in action. On February 8, 1942, Japanese forces crossed the straits leading to Singapore capturing the fortress a week later.

On February 15, 1942, the Japanese invaded Sumatra and the Japanese Premier Hideki Tojo warned that Burma, China, India, the East Indies, Australia, and New Zealand were next, in that order. American and Dutch Naval forces in Java were virtually wiped out. The Japanese bombed Darwin, Australia, for the first time on February 23, 1942, and the Japanese forces were now within reach of Australia

Rangoon fell in mid-February and the Japanese attacked Ceylon and threatened India. The Japanese battle fleet moved into the Bay of Bengal and renewed their threat against Ceylon and India. Easter

167

Sunday, April 1942, marked the end of Japanese expansion at sea. Bataan fell to the Japanese on April 9, 1942, and on May 6, 1942, Corregidor surrendered. The survivors were led on the "Death March" through Manila. General MacArthur had escaped to Australia by PT boat on March 17, 1942.

Bitter resistance in New Guinea slowed the Japanese for the first time. The enemy's defeat at Milne Bay and the following battles for Buna and Gona marked the start of the road back. A Japanese invasion force was defeated in the battle of the Coral Sea on May 2, 1942. It was the first major victory for the United States Navy. By the first week in April, 1942, Japanese land forces were moving along the Kokoda Trail over the Owen Stanley Mountains in an effort to reach Port Moresby where they planned to invade northern Australia. The Japanese naval task force arrived in the Coral Sea on May 2, 1942. Since the American Navy could read the Japanese military codes, they were able to intercept the Japanese fleet in the Coral Sea and defeat the invasion forces before they reached Australia. This defeat of the Japanese Navy was the turning point in the Pacific war and no longer would the Japanese be able to acquire more territory. From this point, on the Japanese forces were on the defensive.

On May 10, 1942, a handful of B-25 Mitchell bombers under the command of Lieutenant Colonel James F. Doolittle dropped bombs on Tokyo, Yokohama, Nagoya and Kobe. In June, 1942, the Japanese Navy was decisively defeated at Midway Island in a greater victory than that of the Coral Sea. On June 3, 1942, the Japanese bombed Dutch Harbor, Alaska, and on June 12, Japanese forces landed in the Aleutian Islands. August 10, Admiral King announced that American troops had landed on the Island of Guadalcanal in the Solomon Islands, which had been invaded by the Japanese earlier in the year. Months of bitter fighting ensued before the enemy was cleared from the islands.

By December 14, 1942, the Japanese were finally driven out of Buna, New Guinea, but they had overrun all of Burma, Thailand, Indo-China, Malay Peninsula, Java, Borneo, the Philippine Islands, the Celebes and the numerous adjoining islands. Enemy troops were firmly entrenched in the entire island of New Guinea. Japanese submarines were operating as Far East as the Pacific coast of the United States, and as far west as Madagascar Island and China.

In 1943, the Allies began the vast pincer movement which was to press the Japanese further and further back towards their home island. With the Allied Forces routing the Japanese from Milne Bay, a leap-frog operation began in1943, traveling up the coast of New Guinea. The purpose of this operation was to jump ahead of the enemy, bypassing many of the enemy troops cutting them off from any support and leaving them to languish in the jungle. By the middle of 1943, the Allies began to gain air superiority, due in part to the ability of the Allies to capture the Japanese airfields as they progressed up the coast of New Guinea.

In 1943, new offensives were being made in India and Burma. American Forces began the clearing of the enemy from the Aleutian Islands. The American Army and Navy forces occupied Amchitka and Adak in the Aleutians and constructed airfields, then bombed Kiska and Attu Islands. In May of 1943, the Army landed on Attu and routed the enemy in three weeks. A subsequent landing on the island of Kiska found the enemy had fled the island.

While the American Navy was engaging the Japanese navy in the Solomon Islands, their submarines were busy. By mid-summer of 1943, they had sunk one third of Japanese shipping. General MacArthur's troops cleared the Huon Peninsula in New Guinea, and then landed troops on New Britain Island. Soon after the landings in New Britain, Allied troops had moved all the way up the northern coast of New Guinea, by-passing many Japanese troops and leaving them cut off from support from the Japanese homeland.

By the summer of 1944, Biak Island, off the northwestern coast of New Guinea, had been captured and secured. The airfields on the island provided the support base needed to enable Allied troops to invade the Philippine Islands. Now General McArthur was in a position to fulfill his promise to the people of the Philippines that he would return.

Many of the younger generation thought that the dropping of the atomic bomb was a terrible thing to do to the Japanese people. But these uninformed and radical thinking people had no idea of what the consequences would have been to have had the bomb and not use it to stop the fighting. With the dropping of the two bombs two cities were demolished and a quarter million people destroyed. Had the atomic bombs not been used, there would have been many more killed and more cities destroyed in the ensuing battle to invade Japan.

Plans were made and all the details were in place to attack the mainland of Japan with five simultaneous amphibious assault landings. Had the war not ended, more than a million troops of the Allies would have been killed. At least another million Japanese troops would have been lost. There is no telling how many Japanese civilians would have perished in the fighting that would have taken place in the cities and towns of Japan.

Even before the actual amphibious assault landings would have been made, the entire countryside would have been torched by fire bombs. The areas where the five landings were to be made would have been bombed into oblivion destroying all the structures and killing all the civilians in those areas.

The nature of the Japanese people and their thinking as Samurais would have forced them to fight to the last man, woman and child. To them, fighting to the death was more desirable than surrendering and losing face. This was demonstrated so many times during the fighting in the war. The Kamikaze pilots were an example of this type of thinking. The young pilots were given their funeral rites before they took off in their planes, since they were not expected to return to their country and their families. The small planes were just a bomb with a motor and wings. There was no thought that the pilot would live to return to his family. He was to sacrifice his life for his family and his Emperor.

The idea of sacrifice for the Emperor was carried out many times during the fighting in the Pacific in what they called a "banzai" charge. The Japanese troops would continue to move into battle and directly attack a gun position knowing that most of them would be

170

killed. They were prepared to either win or all be killed in the attempt. Before the attack they would pledge themselves to fight even though they were wounded. If the battle proved to go against them, they were prepared to disembowel themselves and die rather than surrender and disgrace their family and Emperor.

The Samurai code would have held for the civilians as well as the armed forces of Japan if the Allied Forces had landed on the mainland of Japan. When you hear the members of the generation that was not in the service at the time of World War II, who have no idea of the nature of the Code of the Samurai, say that the A-Bomb should not have been dropped, just remember they know nothing of the situation at that time. Had there been five amphibious assaults on the mainland of Japan and if the A-Bomb had not been dropped there would have been total devastation of the Japanese cities. Millions would have been killed on both sides of the fight.

The signing of the peace treaty with Japan and the cessation of hostilities in Europe did not end the fighting and killing. Colonial unrest in the East Indies began with the end of the war with Japan. Dutch colonies wanted freedom from their oppressors and the right to rule their own people. China continued to fight a civil war between the Nationalists, led by Generalissimo Chiang Kai Shek, and the communists that followed Mao Tse-tung. There was widespread unrest in Indochina and plans were being made to throw off the French yoke of oppression in that country.

In Europe, the Russians were setting up the framework for the start of the cold war that would prevail for almost fifty years. No sooner had the war in Europe ended, than the Russians started to put in place the so-called iron curtain. This would seclude Russia and her puppet nations from the remainder of the world for many years. By no means did World War II stop hostilities all over the world. In fact, it may have been the catalyst for much of the uprisings and conflict following the war. In looking back over the years it seems the shooting and killing never really ceased.

One hundred thousand Chinese Communist troops armed with Japanese weapons marched on Sinkiang Province from the north, east and south. Violence had broken out in the province and there was heavy fighting in Hunan. In October, 1945, the Indonesian Nationalists had challenged the British military intervention in Java.

In Batavia, (now known as Jakarta), British regulars were patrolling the streets to prevent rioting. The interior of Batavia was alive with gangs of native insurgents looting and terrorizing the countryside. An estimated three to four thousand Indonesian casualties were accounted for in just a few weeks. In October, 1945, the revolutionary forces in Venezuela reported they were in complete control of the country.

In Japan, preparations were being made to expedite the trials of Japanese war criminals. Hearings were to be held in Tokyo, and Manila, concurrently. The number of accused persons was in the thousands and there was nothing in the surrender documents to prevent the trial of Emperor Hirohito. During the Japanese occupation of Batangas, in the Philippines, an estimated twenty thousand men, women and children had been mistreated or murdered. Survivors told the story of whole villages being held at gun point by the soldiers while their homes were burned.

After the close of World War II, there was another war to be fought by the Allied Forces against the Communist Forces. Hardly had five years passed when hostilities broke out as North Korean troops overran South Korea. It was not considered a war by the politicians. They called it a "police action". For those that fought there, it was war in its cruelest form. It was the first instance of the "limited area fighting" in which the troops were only allowed to fight where the politicians said it was all right to do so. This forced the troops to wait for the enemy to come to them and the battles were fought on the enemy's terms. After the Korean conflict, there was another limited war or "police action" fought ten years later in Vietnam.

ARTHUR

About the Author

James A. Pounds was born shortly after the close of World War I, and grew up on a subsistence farm in Alabama.

He served in the U.S. Army during World War II in the Southwest Pacific Theater of Operations. He saw combat in New Guinea, Borneo, and the Philippine Islands. He was an Operations Officer in an Amphibious Landing Craft Brigade that made six D-Day-H-Hour landings in the Southwest Pacific.

He was a member of the unit that first served in the Occupation Forces in Japan.

He served as Captain in the United States Army Corps of Engineers in World War II and during the Korean War years.

Made in the USA
Lexington, KY
13 April 2013